THE TRUE
MATCH

Other books by Margaret Carroll:

The Write Match

THE TRUE MATCH

●

Margaret Carroll

AVALON BOOKS
NEW YORK

Published by Thomas Bouregy & Co., Inc.
160 Madison Avenue, New York, NY 10016

Library of Congress Cataloging-in-Publication Data

Carroll, Margaret, 1960–
    The true match / Margaret Carroll.
        p.   cm.
    ISBN 978-0-8034-9883-9 (acid-free paper)
    I. Title.
    PS3603.A774587T78   2008
    813'.6—dc22   2007037200

PRINTED IN THE UNITED STATES OF AMERICA
ON ACID-FREE PAPER
BY HADDON CRAFTSMEN, BLOOMSBURG, PENNSYLVANIA

With all my love to Katie Mae, who thinks I'm the world's best mom, and to my mother, who really is the world's best mom.

Also, to everyone at J-Spa, Rand (for making all my dreams come true, including this one), and heartfelt thanks to T.O.

Chapter One

Hutch the cameraman was tough, and from Texas to boot, so Ruby was as shocked as everyone else when he keeled over.

The Waterford crystal vase that had just sailed across the room and bounced off his head landed on the carpet with a heavy thud.

Ruby winced. "Ooh!"

The vase rolled to a stop. It was in one piece. That was something.

Hutch was lying very still on Ruby's hand-stitched Persian rug from Bloomingdale's.

At least he wasn't bleeding. But maybe using props from Ruby's apartment for the show wasn't such a good idea.

"Somebody, do something! Call nine-one-one!" Wild-eyed, Ruby looked around the set.

1

But nobody was paying attention. Not the woman who had hurled the vase and stormed out. Not the woman's boyfriend, the intended target of the vase, who moments earlier had confessed to cheating on her. Not Colin, the production assistant, who was pleading with them to finish taping.

Which left only Hutch, and he wasn't moving at all.

Ruby frowned. "Darn!" She dropped to her knees at Hutch's side. Even lying down, the man was massive, one large hand still wrapped around his video camera. His lashes lay dark like ebony against his cheeks. His face had turned a scary shade of white.

Ruby's frown deepened. "Hutch!" she called.

No answer.

She clapped her hands so her David Yurman bracelets jangled in Hutch's ear, and her scent, Thierry Mugler's Angel, enveloped him.

His nose twitched, but that was all.

Ruby clapped her hands again. Once, twice, three times. Nothing.

A sliver of fear trickled down her spine, like the first drop of rain preceding a monsoon.

Outside the set, Ruby's talk show guests were arguing with each other in a foreign language. Colin tried to calm them.

Ruby placed one manicured hand on Hutch's chest, which was as rock hard as it looked and cut through with angles like a Calder mobile. Unlike a steel sculpture, however, Hutch's chest was warm and covered in the un-mistakable soft folds of fine Italian cashmere.

Cashmere was an unlikely choice for a man whose main hobbies involved dangling from helicopters under enemy fire and swilling beer.

Ruby sniffed. Keeping her hand in place, she spread her fingers, exploring the tiniest bit.

She noticed something odd.

His chest wasn't moving.

"Oh, no," she whispered. "Help!" she yelled.

But an elevator had arrived, and the group in the hall stepped aboard and left, their shouts fading away behind them.

Which left Ruby alone with Hutch.

The set was now terribly silent.

Ruby gave the cameraman a doubtful look. "Hutch," she whispered.

No reply.

Ruby was motionless for a few seconds, wondering what to do. Until memories of her high school lifeguard training course came flooding back. Not being the sort of girl to sit around and do nothing, she decided some basic lifesaving moves couldn't hurt. Cradling Hutch's head in one hand, she grasped his chin in her other, the way she remembered. More or less.

She took a deep breath, leaned over, and covered Hutch's mouth with hers.

He smelled good, faintly of soap and shaving cream. His lips were firm and warm. His day-old beard felt good on her face, if you liked that *Miami Vice,* Don Johnson sort of thing. Which, Ruby reminded herself, she did not. She blew out a lungful of air with all her might.

The air escaped through Hutch's nose, which she had neglected to pinch shut, a mistake she didn't notice because she was busy straightening her ponytail. She flicked it back, drew in another breath, and got ready to try again.

She blew another breath and waited, sliding her hand down his long throat and onto his chest for balance. Yup. Those pecs managed to be both warm and rock hard at the same time. Now his lips felt firmer, as if they had taken on a life of their own.

Before she knew it, Ruby's lips were moving in response, soft and yielding against his.

She felt Hutch move his free hand—the one without the camera—up her back, gathering her close against him.

Ruby caught her breath.

These were not the final throes of a dying man.

He was coming out of it. In fact, he was making out with her. Charles Begley Hutchinson IV. Ruby's playboy cameraman. Her employee, for heaven's sake.

Ruby pulled back, forgetting the way his mouth had felt on hers, no longer caring whether her ponytail got mussed or not.

Hutch licked his lips like a hungry wolf. His nose twitched. He coughed once, his eyes fluttered open, and his gaze focused on Ruby. He let out a groan and closed them again.

"Well," she snapped, rocking back onto her Kate Spade mules. She gave his shoulder a shake. "Wake up."

Hutch opened one eye and scowled. "It is you, isn't it? For a minute I dreamed I was making love to a beautiful mermaid." His deep baritone voice was husky with pain, which only amplified the effect of his Texas drawl.

Ruby wasn't falling for it. They were now hopelessly behind on their production schedule. She gave him her chilliest glare. "You are hallucinating," she said evenly. "Now, get up."

His lips twitched, calling to mind the term *sardonic grin*. "I liked it better when I was dreaming."

She scowled and offered her hand.

Ignoring it, he tried to rise. And fell back down, wincing in pain.

Ruby's eyes widened in alarm. Hutch, aka the Cowboy Cameraman, was renowned for his willingness to take punishment, even dodge bullets in Iraq, to get the angle he wanted. The man who was so macho that his picture could be found in the dictionary under the letter *M* was now writhing in pain on her wool rug. "Stay there," she ordered. "I'm calling an ambulance."

"Oh, no, you don't. Just give me a couple of aspirin, and I'll be fine." Hutch tried to sit up again and groaned. He sank back down and closed his eyes.

Ruby scrambled for the phone.

"I don't need a dang ambulance," Hutch protested. "I don't want a bunch of doctors making a fuss over a little bump on my head."

Ruby held up one hand. "No arguments. I'm your boss."

Hutch groaned again. "No chance I'd forget that. You remind us all every five minutes."

The smart-alecky smirk on his face told Ruby he didn't

care much about network org charts. He was annoying, no doubt about it. Tough to manage. But she was his boss, after all. So she tightened her lips and mustered her very sternest face, what her father called her Clear-the-Decks look. But "Well, well" was all she could come up with.

A flicker of something lit Hutch's hazel eyes, and his lips twitched all the way from the corners of his muscular jaw to the dimple at the center of his chin.

He was laughing.

At her. The host of cable's newest reality TV show, *Ruby's Relationship Rx.* Obviously, he didn't care one teeny iota that she was his boss. She'd show him. Ruby picked up the red phone that connected directly with the security command post in the lobby. "Hello, operator," she said smoothly, "I need an ambulance right away on Soundstage Three. Somebody has been hurt." She glared at Hutch. "A man who works for me."

Chapter Two

"**Y**ou have a concussion." The attending physician gave Hutch a quick glance and kept writing. Hutch scowled.

The doctor was young and hunky. Unfortunately, the fourth finger of his left hand sported a band of thick, braided gold. Braided bands were OTT—over the top—Ruby thought. A simple plain band was plenty warning enough for any single girl who had popped her contacts in that day.

She yawned. They'd been in the triage unit for hours while Hutch was poked and prodded by the ER staff of St. Clare's Hospital on West Fifty-second Street. All she'd eaten since lunch was a Diet Coke and some stale peanut butter crackers from the vending machine. Definitely not worth the calories.

Dr. Hottie tore a yellow carbon copy from his clipboard

and handed it to Hutch. But he directed his instructions at Ruby.

"Get him home, get him into bed, and keep him quiet. It's okay if he sleeps, but you need to check him every thirty minutes or so for the next twelve hours. If he's unresponsive when you try to wake him, or he starts vomiting, you need to call the triage nurse right away. Got that, Mrs. Hutchinson?"

Mrs. Hutchinson. Ruby's eyes widened. She opened her mouth to set the record straight, but it was too late.

Dr. Hottie was already on his feet. "He'll be fine, and so will you. Don't worry." He flashed her a smile that was meant to be reassuring and turned to go. "Remember, keep him quiet, and check him every thirty minutes or so."

Ruby nodded.

"Someone'll be here to complete your discharge soon. I've gotta run."

He disappeared before Ruby could tell him she was not Mrs. Hutchinson. In fact, she was NYC's most famous bachelorette. Or infamous, depending on which of the tabloids you read. But Dr. Hottie was gone. Leaving Ruby to live with the fact that the best-looking young doctor on New York's West Side was under the mistaken impression that she was married to the curmudgeon on the gurney.

It gave new meaning to the term *health care crisis.*

"Well, that's that." Hutch reached for his denim jacket and swung both feet over the edge of the gurney. "I'll walk you over to Sixth Avenue and get you a cab."

Ruby nodded. For once, she and her annoying cameraman were in complete agreement. The sooner they got into their respective cabs, the sooner this day from *H-E-double-L* would end. She checked her Cartier Oyster tank watch. If they got out of here soon, she could still make it over to Lexington Avenue in time for a martial arts Frē Flō Dō workout at the Equinox gym.

A sound caught her attention. It was the *kerplunk* of a cowboy boot landing on the floor. Hutch had collapsed back onto the pillow before he could even get his boots on.

The sight of Hutch lying there with a hole in one sock might have been comical in other circumstances. But it did not bode well for Ruby's Frē Flō Dō workout. She sighed. She knew the answer to the question she was about to ask, but she asked it anyway. "Is there someone we should call to pick you up?"

Hutch shook his head.

Ruby considered things. Hutch was not only the most sought-after cameraman in the cable network's news division, he was also the most highly paid. Which meant he was not likely to require a roommate to share his stratospheric Manhattan rent. And that fact, at the moment, meant that Ruby might be saddled with him for the rest of the night.

She eyed him. A man like Hutch, with his long, tall Texas build and Brad Pitt jaw, not to mention those light hazel eyes, was bound to have a girlfriend somewhere in the five boroughs. Probably any number of girlfriends. It was worth a try. "Girlfriend?"

He didn't respond.

Not that Ruby cared whether Hutch had a girlfriend or not. But his strong, silent routine was wearing thin. "Well, somebody needs to meet you at your apartment," she said finally.

"Nope." He made no move to pull his boots on, only stared resolutely at a spot on the celling. His face was as white as the hospital-issue sheets, minus the blue embroidered script that read *St. Clare's Hospital.*

Ruby's vision of a workout did a quick fade. She looked at Hutch, exasperated. "You're in no shape to go home alone."

The set of his jaw hardened from just plain stubborn to something that looked as if it had been carved in granite on the side of Mount Rushmore. "I need some fresh air, is all. I'll be fine."

"Okay, then. I'll just have to take you to your place myself."

A look of genuine alarm spread across Hutch's face. "Let's not get crazy here. I'm okay. A good night's sleep and I'll be as good as new. I've been cooped up here all afternoon and half the night, and it was a waste of time." He shot her an accusing glance.

"Coming here was the right thing to do," Ruby said firmly. "You heard the doctor. You have a concussion."

"Which is a fancy way of saying I've got a lump on my head."

"Which you got because you didn't duck in time."

Hutch's hazel eyes flashed. "Which I got because you riled that poor woman up so badly, she wanted to knock her boyfriend's block off."

Ignoring him, Ruby fished around in her Birkin bag for her compact. She surveyed herself in the mirror and sighed. Fluorescent lights were the enemy. Why, she wondered, could hospitals not install full-spectrum lighting? It would lift people's spirits and speed their recovery. Someone should do a study on that, she thought, lining her lips with a neutral mauve-y shade before painting on a layer of matte lipstick with a small brush. She topped it off with sheer gloss from a tiny pot. She accomplished all this in a matter of seconds while Hutch watched, a mixture of curiosity and admiration on his face.

"You'd be good on a road trip," he observed. "You're organized. I like that in a woman."

A man who could make a pass at his boss from a supine position in a hospital bed was just plain Arrogant—capital *A*. He needed straightening out, Ruby decided. "Let's stay on topic, shall we? First, it's my job to get people talking about the issues they need to resolve in their relationship. Or, as you say, 'riled up.' " She paused for effect. But the effort seemed to be wasted on Hutch, who was staring at the ceiling again. "Second, I show them how to fix those issues. So they can have better relationships. That is why I have my own show." *And you don't,* she did not add.

Hutch let loose a sound from deep in his throat that qualified as a guffaw. "You don't really think you helped that couple today, do you?"

Ruby raised one perfectly arched eyebrow.

"You backed that poor guy so far into a corner, he fessed up to taking his old girlfriend out to dinner."

"He's practically married already," Ruby shot back.

"He took an old friend to dinner. One time," Hutch said with a shrug. "It meant nothing."

Ruby's eyes widened in disbelief. "It meant every-thing! He takes his old girlfriend to dinner behind his girl-friend's back when they're practically engaged? That's a crime that should be punishable by law."

"Apparently, his girlfriend agreed," Hutch said, rub-bing his skull thoughtfully. "She had quite an arm too."

Ruby checked her reflection in her compact and gave her nose a quick dab with a powder puff. "He deserved it."

"Maybe." Hutch shrugged. "But the point is, your show is supposed to keep couples together, not tear them apart."

He was right. Today had been a disaster even before Hutch got bonked. Ruby stopped dabbing and looked at him.

"Look," Hutch leaned forward, warming to his subject. "One dinner with a guy's old girlfriend doesn't mean any-thing. You have to consider it from the male point of view."

Ruby rolled her eyes. In her experience, whenever a man suggested she consider things from the "male point of view," she was about to get a heavy load of snow shov-eled her way. Big-time.

Hutch was just getting warmed up. "See, the thing is, the guy did it for old times' sake. He knows he's about to spend the rest of his life with the new girlfriend. He just wanted to see somebody from his past, take a look back at the life he's about to close the door on. His ex doesn't mean anything to him. If she did, he'd be with her." Hutch paused, waiting to see if Ruby got it.

As though it was vitally important that Ruby come to a deep understanding of the great, mysterious Guy Point of View.

Blinking once, Ruby gave a tight smile. "Oo-kay."

His response was to utter the two words Ruby had vowed never to believe again, at least not when they issued forth from a male mouth. "Trust me."

Ruby snapped her compact shut. "Yeah."

Hutch winced. To his credit, he seemed to sense when he'd lost his audience. He shook his head. "Baby, I'm just telling you the way it is. From a guy's point of view."

Baby. Ruby stood six feet tall even in her pantyhose, with long blond hair and regal looks that could stop a cab at rush hour in the rain. She had steel blue eyes and blood to match, born and bred in Great Neck, on Long Island's famed Gold Coast.

She had never been called *baby* in her life.

But the way the word rolled off Hutch's lips, as easy and smooth as a mint julep on a hot Texas day, made her stomach do a flip-flop the way it did when she was at the very top of a roller coaster.

Ruby hated roller coasters.

She leveled her steely eyes at Hutch. "At least our philandering boyfriend managed to duck in time."

Something glinted in Hutch's eyes, like a dark shadow flitting through a field of sagebrush.

Some women would find his smoldering good looks attractive, even sexy. But Ruby was not one of them. No. Hutch had been assigned to work on her show only until the shrapnel wounds in his leg healed. Then he would return to his real job, shooting battle footage of the 101st Airborne Division in Kirkuk, Iraq, for the network's round-the-clock news channel.

"I got hit in the course of doing my job," Hutch replied, his voice dropping a notch into the danger zone. "A cameraman isn't worth much if he doesn't bring back the shot. And I always get mine."

Ruby could think of nothing to say to that, so she studied the pointy tips of her green snakeskin mules against the mottled white linoleum floor. After a while she snuck another glance at Hutch, who was attempting to sit up again.

He met her gaze, and she was relieved to see that his eyes had shifted back to a sunnier shade of hazel.

He rolled with the punches; that was something.

"You'll be happy to know I kept the camera rolling. I got the shot."

Ruby brightened. "Really?"

Hutch leaned over the edge of the bed, wrestling with his cowboy boots again. When he spoke, his voice was tight. "Yup. Got it all. Cussin', swearin', cryin', even that vase coming my way in midair. There's your money shot."

She smiled. "Well done." Hutch was, after all, known as the Cowboy Cameraman for his ability to stay cool under fire.

He managed to get his boots on at last and stood. But he was none too steady, his face still as pinched and white as those hundred-thread–count polyester sheets.

An orderly arrived with a wheelchair.

Hutch waved him off. "I don't need that."

"Hospital policy, sir," the orderly replied.

"I can walk," Hutch said. He took a step to prove his point—and swayed.

Ruby managed to get one arm under his shoulders just

as the orderly wheeled the chair into place underneath him. Hutch teetered long enough for Ruby to notice how tall he was. Not to mention that those big shoulders were surprisingly comfortable when you were standing beneath them. And he smelled good, piney and clean.

He landed smoothly, managing to keep one arm tightly around the small of Ruby's back so that his hand came to rest in the narrow part of her waist. As if he owned her.

She looked at him and arched an eyebrow.

He winked and eased his arm off, slow and gentle, leaving a trail of warmth on the small of her back, till she was left holding his hand. Which was surprisingly warm and comfortable.

"There you go, sir." The orderly propped Hutch's boot-clad feet into position on the footrests. "Now you and your wife can get on your way."

Ruby and Hutch raised their voices together and protested as one. "We're not married!"

The orderly shrugged as they set off. "Okay, folks, this way out."

Thanks to Hutch's getting hit with that vase, they were one day behind on production. If he didn't make a speedy recovery, tomorrow would make it two. Not good. That settled things for Ruby. She'd take him to his place, tuck him into bed, and wait there till his girlfriend showed up. She'd skip her spinning class tonight too, but it would be worth it to keep the show on track.

Hutch's apartment was different than she expected. He lived in Tudor City, a quaint collection of red brick buildings tucked away on several leafy side streets just west of the UN. The building lobby wasn't chic, but it was warm and inviting. The doorman gave them a cheery greeting but didn't bat an eye at Ruby.

That struck her as odd, since most men craned their necks to get a better look. She was registered with *FRESH,* the modeling agency that had launched a thousand faces. The fact that the doorman didn't ogle her was an indication that Hutch's apartment probably got more traffic than the Long Island Expressway during rush hour.

Inside, his place was clean and neat. The living room offered a charming view of the East River from the double set of casement windows and was furnished with what looked to be antiques of exceptional quality. No chrome or glass in sight, not even the standard-issue bachelor's leather couch. An occasional table in a corner caught her eye. "Biedermeier?"

Hutch only nodded in reply. He was too busy struggling to stay upright to pay much attention. He was starting to tilt.

Ruby dropped her Birkin bag and managed to slide one arm underneath his just in time. "Where's your bedroom?"

He looked down at her and grinned.

More of a leer, actually.

"Normally, I'd take you to dinner first," he said in that drawl of his.

Ruby felt her cheeks flame just the tiniest bit. Which was ridiculous. She never blushed. And she wasn't about to start now. "Thanks," she said, keeping her tone as cool and smooth as fresh-churned butter. "But I don't much care for burgers and beer."

He laughed, a low, easy rumbling from deep in his chest. "I was thinking ribs, if you want to know the truth."

Ruby wrinkled her nose and tried to ignore how—well—how solid Hutch felt around his middle.

He misread her silence. "Oh, I get it. You're watching your calories." He said the last word slowly, drawing out the *a* in *calories* with his best Texas accent, and grinned.

If he was healthy enough to make fun of her, he was strong enough to walk on his own. Ruby took her arm back.

They shuffled down the short hall to the bedroom, Hutch narrating as they went in that smooth baritone of his. He flipped on an heirloom Stiffel lamp. "See, you New Yorkers have a thing or two to learn when it comes to eating. Take your basic barbecue. That's what we call it, by the way. Not barbecued ribs or barbecued steak, just barbecue." He checked to make sure she was listening and flashed another smile when he saw that she was.

"You have your collard greens, which are chock-full of iron, vitamin C, and no calories to speak of. I know that's what you're after, but if you don't mind my saying so, you shouldn't worry so much about that. And then you have your grits. There's nothing better than a side of grits to round out a meal. Big plate of grits would do you some good."

It was rare to find a man bold enough to tell a woman she needed to put on weight. Rarer still if the man in question was telling it to his boss. And here he was, acting as if she had come up to his place for a nightcap, for heaven's sake. "I'll keep that in mind," Ruby said tightly.

Battered equipment cases lined the room, scattered among classic pieces of gleaming Baker mahogany. But the centerpiece was a gleaming antique brass bed, neatly covered with an heirloom-quality quilt in a classic pattern. Interlocking wedding bands.

Curious.

Hutch had already propped himself up against the pillows and was busy pulling his boots off. That done, he smiled at her, revealing rows of large white teeth that were a perfect complement to his skin, which, thankfully, had returned to a shade of tan.

With those looks, Ruby thought idly, he could sign on with *FRESH* and become a model, maybe sell Hummers or chain saws or speedboats or something. The thought made her aware she was in a strange man's bedroom. She crossed her arms. And then uncrossed them, not wanting to seem prissy. "Well," she said briskly, "I doubt I can find you any grits, but I can order in Chinese. How about that?"

His grin deepened till he looked like the Cheshire cat as he swung his long legs up onto the bed and settled himself more deeply into the pillows. "Sounds good to me. Dinner in bed with a beautiful woman. Almost makes the lump on my head worthwhile."

He was enjoying this too much. Ruby's eyes narrowed. "Lucky for you, you've got a thick skull."

He let loose another laugh from deep inside that cashmere sweater. "You're right about that, Ruby."

Ruby. His southern drawl lengthened her name, adding another whole syllable. It sounded sexy, a fact that registered as a small bounce against the walls deep inside her solar plexus. She overrode the bouncy feeling by turning on her Kate Spades and heading out the door.

"Take-out menus are in the kitchen drawer," he called after her.

They dined on his bed, atop a tablecloth Ruby spread to protect that wedding band quilt, which turned out to be handmade.

"Somebody did a beautiful job," she observed, nibbling a bite of steamed broccoli, sans sauce.

Hutch swallowed. "My mother and her quilting group made it." He used his chopsticks to spear another piece of General Tso's Chicken, which probably had a million calories per bite.

"It's lovely." Impressed, Ruby traced one long finger along the small, even stitches. She couldn't sew a button if her life depended on it. "It must have taken years."

"Not quite. They finished in ten months, just in time for my—" Hutch stopped and got busy tearing open a packet of soy sauce, the kind that was loaded with sodium.

"Just in time for your what?" Ruby's eyes narrowed as she studied the interlocking wedding band pattern. An interesting choice as a gift from mother to bachelor son.

Hutch didn't answer. He shoveled a large bite of chicken into his mouth so fast, he nearly lost a chopstick.

Which strengthened Ruby's suspicion that Charles Begley Hutchinson IV, once upon a time, might have been a groom. But the story did not have a fairy-tale ending. Not at all. Not if he was sleeping alone beneath that quilt. Which meant that his wedding had been called off. He was the guilty party—Ruby was sure of it. No bride ever canceled her own wedding. Not when things had progressed to the handmade quilt stage.

Hutch was a man. And therefore the enemy. Ruby's lightly steamed snow pea pods turned to garden weeds in her mouth. She set her chopsticks down. "I understand. That quilt was meant to be a wedding gift."

Hutch gulped. Audibly. He looked like someone caught in the center of a crosswalk after the light turns red.

Ruby pursed her lips. "No need to explain." She sat still, waiting for him to explain.

Hutch's tan faded a bit, and he was silent for a long moment. "I was engaged once, a long time ago," he said finally. "We never made it to the altar. At least there were no lawyers involved."

"So, in other words, no big deal." Ruby's tone was acid.

"I wouldn't say that," Hutch began as Ruby stood.

She gathered the containers of food.

"Hey, I wasn't finished with my General Tso's," he protested.

Ruby scooped it up.

"We didn't even read our fortune cookies." Hutch reached for a cookie, but Ruby snatched it away.

"I don't think sweets are the right thing for you now, after the day you've had."

"Aw, come on, Ruby, don't go all hard on me. Just because your—" He was about to say something but stopped short when he saw the look on her face.

Ruby went still. A package of hot mustard slid to the floor. "Just because my what?"

Hutch looked out the window, where a tugboat inched its way up the East River. "Never mind."

"Never mind what?"

Ruby's temper was known around the set of *Ruby's Relationship Rx,* so Hutch probably saw what was coming.

Ruby felt her alabaster cheeks heat up as her lips formed a pout. The skin on top of her delicate knuckles lost color as she tightened her grip on the takeout containers.

Watching her, Hutch sighed. "Look, Ruby, everybody knows you got a raw deal, but what happened to you and what happened to me are two different things."

Ruby fingered the takeout containers and wondered how Hutch would look with a quart of General Tso's chicken dumped on his head. Somewhere in Texas, Hutch's ex-girlfriend would get a warm, tingly feeling and not know why—Ruby was certain of it.

As though he sensed her thoughts, Hutch raised a hand in protest. "Now, Ruby girl, you just calm yourself. No need to get all worked up over something that's over and done with."

His tone was calm, soothing. Like that of the ski instructor who had coached her down the Ajax Mountain mogul field last winter in Aspen. Like that of a man who had tons of experience with distraught women, Ruby thought sourly.

"Look." Hutch's voice dropped a notch. "I know you went through a bad time, getting ditched at the altar at the last minute. It was in all the papers. It must have been rough."

Ruby swallowed hard around the lump that rose in her throat. It had been rough. Her fiancé had discovered the woman of his dreams practically ten minutes before he was scheduled to walk up the aisle with Ruby. Ruby canceled the reception and returned the ring. That was the easy part. The part that took longer was accepting the fact that her ex-fiancé had not been the Right One. Her True Match was out there, Ruby was certain. She just hadn't met him yet.

She had promised herself she would take a year off from dating. She was six months into it, and she wasn't about to forget the promise she had made to herself, not even if Hutch's eyes had just gone soft and his shoulders looked plenty big enough to rest her head on. Nope. Ruby had other fish to fry. Namely, making a name for herself with her new cable TV show that would make everyone forget she was the woman who had been dubbed Gotham's "Jilted Bride" by the tabloid press.

Hutch was still watching her with those big doe eyes. He made a move in her direction, bringing his broad shoulders with him.

Ruby was tempted to let her guard down. But a promise was a promise, especially if that promise was made to one-self. Not to mention that Hutch was one of Them. A Man. Ruby cleared her throat, sat up very straight, and shot him her best All-We've-Got-between-Us-Is-Business look.

Hutch drew back.

The man could take a hint—Ruby would give him that much.

He sighed. "I guess we've both been hurt. But what I

did and what your fiancé did are two different things. I think we need to forget all about it and declare a truce. Deal?" He offered his hand.

The aroma of General Tso's secret sauce tickled Ruby's nose. Her fingers itched to dump the container over his head, just to even the score in case he was a handsome cad who had jilted some poor girl long ago and was lying about it now. But piling anything else on top of Hutch's thick skull wouldn't do his concussion any good, and, worse, it might add another delay to Ruby's production schedule. Her producer would have a hard time finding another cameraman on short notice, thereby slowing Ruby's meteoric rise to stardom.

Ruby loosened her grip on the General Tso's and forced a smile to her lips. "Deal."

They shook on it.

She stowed the leftovers in the fridge, which was crowded with packages of thirty-five–millimeter film and not much else. Orange juice past its sell-by date, soda crackers, half a wedge of crumbling Saga blue cheese, a six-pack of Bud, and a bottle of surprisingly good quality French champagne.

She made her way to the bathroom, stopping to check on Hutch. In his sleep, he looked peaceful, even harmless. Ruby reminded herself that even convicted felons probably looked peaceful when they slept.

The bathroom was spotless. A worn toiletry kit hung from the back of the door, ready to be rolled up and crammed into Hutch's duffel bag at a moment's notice. The medicine cabinet yielded just one item of interest among the usual sundries, a pot of Prescriptives lip gloss—Dark Honey—that smelled ancient and looked to have been abandoned some time ago. There was a pile of freshly laundered plush towels, along with a coordinating bath mat. And, best of all, an unopened container of bath salts. Ruby broke the seal and sprinkled some into the deep, cast-iron soaking tub, just one of the touches of luxury from bygone days, when Tudor City was built as affordable housing for GIs returning from WWII.

The hot soak restored her. She toweled off and eyed her clothing. The thought of putting it back on did not appeal to her. A dark blue flannel robe hung from a hook, and she chose that instead. She slid into it. It was cozy and about twenty sizes too big, but it felt like heaven. The scent of pine and, well, man, floated up to her nose, and, to tell the truth, it was a good smell. She brushed out her ponytail and let her long hair spill around her shoulders. Ruby felt restored.

She checked on Hutch. He was more cooperative than she'd expected, even half-asleep. He woke up long enough to mumble his thanks before drifting back to sleep. Kind of sweet.

She checked the time. Just after ten. Too early to turn in. She collected a bottle of spring water from the kitchen and took a long swig. Ruby drank twelve glasses of water every day to keep her skin hydrated.

She wandered out to the living room, restless. There was nothing to watch on the ancient TV. The coffee table held a few back issues of *National Geographic* and that was all.

On the floor were two big cartons covered with JFK bar

code stickers and Arabic writing. The seal across the top
of each was broken.

Practically an invitation to look.

Inside were stacks and stacks of black-and-white pho-
tographs, organized into groups, each with a contact
sheet labeled in grease pencil. Ruby flipped through them
quickly at first, but the images were so haunting, she forgot everything else and sat cross-legged on the floor so
she could study them.

There were dozens and dozens of shots of a landscape
she recognized from the nightly news as the rugged desert
region of northern Iraq. But she had never seen it like this,
captured in still frame so the light played across the dust
on the ancient hills and told the story of the place at every
hour of the day. There were many different series, captur-
ing the look of the land in each season and every kind of
weather, day and night. The shivering cold and blistering
heat practically radiated from each photo.

The most captivating, however, were the portraits. People of all ages. The camera captured their faces, etched
with emotions as stark as the land around them. People
going about their daily routines. Some tended flocks of
livestock; some stood in the doorways of homes made of
concrete. Others posed in the wreckage of buildings that
had been bombed. Their faces told their stories. A few
smiled, many were full of fear, and some had eyes that
burned with anger. The camera captured it all.

A sound from the doorway made Ruby turn.

Hutch watched her, in a pair of sweats and a T-shirt
from Ron-Ton's Surf Shop in Florida.

With his dark hair, light eyes, and sparkling teeth, he could be a poster boy for the Sunshine State, Ruby thought.

"I see you found my still photos," he said.

Ruby looked down. "I tripped over the boxes, and some of the pictures fell out." Lie.

Hutch gave a mighty stretch, revealing ripples of muscle across his stomach and arms. "Feel free to poke around. I see you found my robe too. Looks a lot better on you than it does on me."

Now Ruby felt the heat of a full-on blush in her cheeks. She couldn't think of a clever comeback, so she remained silent, tightening the belt on his robe in an effort to appear more dignified than she felt. "The photos are terrific," she said finally, changing the subject. "I didn't know you shot stills."

"Just on my free time, when I'm on assignment."

"I've never seen anything like them," Ruby said, meaning it. "You should have them published."

"Thanks." He ducked his head and looked away, and it occurred to Ruby that he was uncomfortable with compliments. He reached for another stack that was filled with shots of a country bazaar, with bustling market stalls filled to capacity with every item imaginable, from yards of patterned fabric to barrels of grain. He found what he was looking for and handed it to her with a smile. "Shoe shopping. Right up your alley."

The photo was of a stall crammed top to bottom with sandals made of rubber and hemp, the kind Charlton Heston wore in *Ben-Hur*.

Ruby laughed. "You don't know me well enough to say that."

There was a mischievous gleam in his eye. "Oh, but I do. For instance, you've got enough hardware on your wrists to trigger alarms at every airport security checkpoint I've ever been through."

Her eyes widened. "How did you know? Last time I flew from LaGuardia, they hand-searched me. I almost missed my plane."

Hutch grinned. "Glad I wasn't in line behind you."

"Anybody should be able to recognize genuine David Yurman when they see it." She jangled her bracelets for emphasis.

Hutch frowned. "Don't tell me you got a security guard who didn't have his Tiffany certificate?"

Ruby perked up at the mention of the store that was hallowed ground for brides-to-be everywhere. "Tiffany certificate?"

"Sure. The FAA offers a special course in jewelry identification. They take them to Tiffany to show them how to spot the genuine article. You should have been fast-tracked right through security." Hutch reached for Ruby's hand and pulled it close so he could examine her bracelets. The rest of her arm followed.

His hand was warm on hers, his touch gentle as he slid his fingers along the length of her arm, touching her skin. "Oh yeah," he murmured, his voice dropping a notch, "this is the real McCoy, all right."

She looked into his eyes. Up close she could see flecks

of gold mixed in with the hazel, like rays of sunshine that made her warm all over.

His eyes twinkled.

A suspicious thought came to mind, causing Ruby to catch her breath. "I've never heard of jewelry identification training for airport security guards."

Hutch's lips twitched.

She made a move to tug her hand back, but not very hard. "There's no such thing as a Tiffany certificate, is there?"

Now Hutch was grinning like the Cheshire cat, his shoulders shaking as he let loose a full laugh. "'Fraid not."

Knowing he'd gotten the better of her, Ruby tried to purse her lips. But it was no use. She giggled. "Well, they should."

"Would make life easier for you, wouldn't it?" He was laughing out loud now.

Ruby knew he was poking fun at her, and she should be bothered. But his eyes were so warm with that light from inside, not to mention the heat of his hand on hers. And right then he pulled her, it seemed, the tiniest bit closer to him.

Ruby smiled. "You're making fun of me."

His expression turned serious, even though the corners of his eyes still crinkled like Matthew McConaughey's. "I'm teasing you, is all. I'd never, ever make fun of you, Ruby." His voice dropped a notch, sending shivers up and down Ruby's spine.

She felt her stomach turn to mush, and this time she was certain he was pulling her closer, into his arms. His eyelids drooped, and she knew what people meant when they talked about "bedroom eyes."

One more inch and she would have another close encounter with those hungry lips.

But they were interrupted by the sound of a key turning in the lock.

Chapter Three

The front door opened, and there was Kristal, Hutch's on-again, off-again girlfriend.

Hutch felt his blood run cold.

"Hey, handsome! I got off work early." Kristal's smile did a quick fade once she got a gander at Ruby, who was practically sitting on Hutch's lap.

The temperature of Hutch's blood plummeted to somewhere around freezing.

Kristal was her stage name. She worked the late shift at the Golden Globes, a bar known for its dazzling showbiz theme and waitresses to match. Hutch stopped in occasionally for a beer on his way home from work. The place was tucked away under the entrance to the Fifty-ninth Street Bridge and had a friendly feel.

There was no *esprit de corps* in the air right now, however. Not from Kristal, whose eyes were shooting sparks to match the sequins on her leotard. And not from Ruby, who had gone as stiff as a board.

There went the night. Timing was key, Hutch thought sadly. Kristal had chosen the worst possible moment to let herself into his apartment. Hutch released his hold on Ruby's arm and scrambled to his feet.

He tried to keep his tone light. Nothing wrong here. "Hey there, Kristal, I can explain."

He heard a hiss escape from Ruby behind him, but he didn't dare turn to look. His gut told him to keep his eyes peeled in front, where his sometime gal pal stood, arms akimbo as she drew in a deep breath.

Gathering wind, no doubt, for the long monologue wherein she would tell him exactly what she thought of him. Hutch raised a hand to head her off. "Kristal, please . . ."

Kristal took a step closer. There was gum in her mouth, and she cracked it. Loudly.

The sound moved through Hutch like a rifle shot.

"No excuses. I'm not in the mood." Kristal's voice rose a notch.

Dang. Girls like Kristal were hard to come by. She commuted in from Brooklyn to work the night shift at the club. On weekends she entertained at private parties. Which meant she had very little free time, even for talking on the phone. Not to mention the Golden Globes. In short, Kristal was the perfect girlfriend. He'd hate to lose her. Hutch made a quick decision to play the sympathy card. It was a cheap shot, but it was his best one. "I got hurt really badly at work and had to go to the hospital."

"Oh, and I suppose *she's* here to provide physical therapy." Kristal jabbed a finger in Ruby's direction.

Uh-oh. Now Ruby got riled and stepped out from behind Hutch to set the record straight. "Actually, I'm his boss."

Hutch swallowed a groan. But it was too late. The damage was done.

"Oh, really?" Kristal's voice was sticky with sarcasm. "And what department are you in charge of, men's pajamas?"

It was a rhetorical question, so Hutch hoped Ruby wouldn't answer.

But ol' Ruby was not one to dodge an issue. She pulled the sash on Hutch's robe tightly and stood up straight and tall. Even though this was not the time to be thinking about such things, Hutch couldn't help but notice that Ruby did have a tiny waist. And her blue eyes were even prettier when they flashed, like now.

"I'll have you know that I have my own TV show," Ruby began evenly.

"So did Anna Nicole Smith!" Kristal shot back.

Ruby gasped.

Kristal turned to Hutch. "Now, let's see. What was your excuse the last time?" She put one index finger to her chin as though she was lost in thought.

But Hutch knew Kristal had a memory like an elephant, and he winced at what was coming next.

"Let's see, last time it was a friend from college who couldn't find a hotel room. And the time before that, it was a lady plumber who was soaking in the tub in search of a leaky pipe, and the time before that . . ."

Ruby harrumphed, and Hutch knew that if Kristal kept this up, he would need to finish recuperating at the unemployment office. Anger spread among women like a prairie wildfire on a windy day. It was time to play a different card. Hutch took a tentative step in Kristal's direction. "Listen, sugar, you got it all wrong. Besides, I don't deserve you, anyway."

"You got that right," Kristal snapped.

"That's right," Ruby echoed, her voice frosty.

What a shame, Hutch thought. Until a few short moments ago, the night had been filled with possibilities. Such as the opportunity to get to know his sexy new boss much, much better. Now that didn't seem likely anytime in the near future. Not to mention that he was about to lose his on-again, off-again sure-thing-on-a-weeknight gal pal, Kristal. His best strategy now was to limit collateral damage, nothing more. "It's not you. It's me," Hutch began in his most sincere tone. "I'm not good enough for you."

"You can say that again," Kristal snapped, raising herself to her full height so her sequins shimmied.

At least she wasn't crying. Kristal was not the sentimental type. Hutch felt a flood of relief. "I'm sorry, Kristal, but you deserve better," he said. He was not above groveling if it would cut this scene short.

"You got that right," Kristal snapped again.

"You go, girl," Ruby chimed in.

Uh-oh. Ruby was warming to the subject. Not good. He was beginning to worry that Kristal and Ruby would come together in an Oprah moment, share a hug, and bond over their disdain for him and for all *man*kind.

Thankfully, Ruby stayed put.

Kristal was busy working Hutch's key off her key ring. "We're through!" She yanked the door open and turned. "Take your key, and, well, you just know what!" She flung it at Hutch.

Hutch caught this one in time. It had been a bad day for throwing things, he thought.

Kristal slammed the door as she left.

The room was now too quiet for Hutch's liking. He drew in a deep breath and took his time letting it out, stalling. He suddenly felt tired and achy all over. He showed Ruby his best hangdog look. "Sorry you had to see that."

Ruby was back in diva mode. She was busy twisting the belt on his robe into a knot and then knotting it again for good measure. "Not at all," she said, using the tone she used at work, all business. "I think it helps us get to know each other. So we know where we stand."

"Oh, come on now, Ruby girl." Hutch made a move in her direction, but one look at her face stopped him. Those blue eyes of hers, so soft and yielding just a short time ago, had turned to little cubes of ice. And her lips, so soft and full that he could practically taste their honey, were now arranged into a tight, thin line.

"You must be exhausted, what with all you've got going on," she said.

As though she figured he had so many women around, he barely had time to sleep. Shoot. The fact was, Hutch was the king of casual dating. A serial dater, one of his gal pals had once called him, and she hadn't meant it as a compliment. He didn't have a special someone. Hadn't in years. Not since he almost took the plunge. And that had been a blazin' fiasco. The memory of it even now made him squeeze his eyes shut.

Ruby saw it and homed right in. "I see how tired you are," she said, still in full Boss Lady mode. "I suggest you get some rest. You're going to need it. Because we've got a full day on the set tomorrow."

Hutch opened his eyes and gave her his best, deep, smoldering look, the one that reduced most women to putty. He waited for a few seconds to see if it would work.

Nothing. Nada. Zip.

Ruby stared at him, arms crossed. She was a handful, used to getting her own way. Trouble. The kind of woman who ate men for breakfast. But Hutch couldn't help himself. The fact was, Charles Begley Hutchinson IV rarely met a woman he could resist, and Ruby Lattingly was no exception. In fact, she'd hit him harder than most. Much harder, if he was truthful about it. "Aw, Ruby, give me a chance to explain."

"No need." She took a deep swig from her water bottle.

"I thought we had a moment there," Hutch began.

She pulled the Evian bottle from her mouth so fast, her pouty lips made a popping sound. " 'A moment'? You think we had 'a moment'?" Her pale eyebrows drew closely together above that pretty little turned up nose. "You see, Hutch, that's what I mean. You need to get some rest." She smiled sweetly. "Because you are delirious."

One thing Hutch had learned growing up with seven sisters: when a woman was finished with him. And that was that. He massaged the lump on his head, trying to push away the memory of how easily his hands had parted those chic bracelets to find the soft skin of Ruby's forearm. "Okay, Ruby girl, I'll just settle myself here on the couch. You go make yourself at home in my bed." The couch wasn't nearly long enough to accommodate his six-foot four-inch frame. Hutch couldn't help but hope Ruby would insist he recuperate in his great big brass bed.

But she was already gone, slamming the bedroom door behind her.

Chapter Four

Ruby spent a restless night, awakened every thirty minutes by the alarm on her BlackBerry so she could stumble out to the couch and check on Hutch.

She dreamed of Texas, a place she had never been, where the sun shone brightly on endless plains. Tumbleweeds bumped along in a space that stretched into eternity. She felt rather than heard a fluttering, a delicate gathering of energy that spoke to her of something soft and featherlight. And then, when she was on the edge of sleep, it was gone.

Ruby came to with a frown, struggling to remember her dream. But it disappeared like a wisp of warm air, lost in the sounds of traffic that floated up from the FDR Drive below. The traffic sounds were familiar, from good ol' New York. The bed was not. She was in a strange bed. Hutch the cameraman's bed.

Yikes!

She threw back the covers and jumped out of bed, onto the parquet floor. The clock radio glowed, showing it was almost seven. The night was over. Thank goodness.

Ruby dressed, splashed water onto her face in the bathroom, and eyed Hutch's toothbrush. It brought to mind his wide, sunny smile, those lips that had felt hard and warm all at the same time when they closed on hers yesterday. The Cowboy Cameraman who was not at all her type. Ruby scowled. She squeezed toothpaste onto her index finger instead and did the best she could.

The scent of coffee drifted from the tiny kitchen. Hutch was already up and dressed, loading fresh oranges into a juicer. He smiled and wiped his hands on his jeans when he saw her. "Mornin', sunshine. Coffee's on. I got us bagels from Tal's. They're still warm."

Ruby's mouth watered. Tal's on Second Avenue had the best bagels in midtown. It was very considerate of him to get up early and organize breakfast. She felt herself soften. Then she reminded herself that this was the man who had given his spare key to a woman who dressed in a sequined leotard for work. Not to mention those interlocking wedding bands on his quilt.

Hutch was a Class A womanizer, no doubt about it. "Thanks, anyway. I don't do breakfast."

He cocked his head, surveying her from top to bottom. "Wouldn't do you any harm."

"I prefer to hit the ground running," she replied crisply.

He grinned. "I'll just bet you do. Listen, Ruby, thank you for looking after me. And I'm sorry you had to meet—"

She cut him off. "Don't be silly." The words came out with more of an edge than she'd intended. The last thing she wanted to do was leave Hutch with the impression that she cared whether he had a girlfriend or not. "It's no big deal."

Hutch raised a hand reflexively to the lump on his head and rubbed it. "Right," he said simply.

"We've got some time to make up. I'll see you on the set, if you're up for it." He had been injured on the job, after all.

"I'm up for it."

"Good." She turned to go. There was a lot riding on the success of her new show, not to mention that she had a meeting with her producer later in the day.

Hutch insisted on coming down to hail her a cab, despite the fact that she was a native New Yorker and perfectly capable of getting her own taxi. But there was something sweet about his insistence. Maybe it was the way his hand rested lightly on her elbow all the way down the steps from Tudor City to Dag Hammarskjöld Plaza, or maybe it was the UN gardens at this hour, oozing peace and tranquility from across First Avenue. The East River sparkled like jewels in the morning sun. Whatever. Ruby felt good.

They found a cab, and Ruby settled herself in the backseat. The radio was tuned to New York's one and only country music station. It was playing, of all things, the old Mitch Miller version of "Yellow Rose of Texas."

Excited, Ruby turned to tell Hutch, but the taxi was already pulling away.

He watched her from the sidewalk with a pensive look

on his face, one she hadn't seen before. Catching her eye, he gave a small nod.

As though they had come to some sort of understanding.

"Hmmph," Ruby muttered, settling back against the seat as the cab sped north.

The "Yellow Rose of Texas" played in her head for the rest of the day.

Later, on the set, Hutch made no mention of the fact that Ruby had spent the night at his place.

Thank goodness.

"That's quite a lump you've got," Colin, the production assistant for the show, observed.

Hutch simply shrugged.

Colin handed Ruby a large container of iced coffee. "You'd better take a sip of this. You're going to need it."

"Thanks." Ruby closed her lips around the straw, careful not to smudge her lipstick. Colin was one of her closest friends since college days, which had its benefits. Such as, he knew how she liked her coffee, with a dollop of skim and two packets of Sweet 'n Low.

"Here you go, boss," Colin handed her a copy of the the *New York Post*.

Ruby's stomach did the thing it did on roller coasters, just when the car began its drop from the top of the highest hill.

Ruby hated roller coasters.

She knew without asking which page to look at. Page Six. The gossip column.

There it was:

Ouch! That's gotta hurt! *Things got off to a bumpy start on the first day of filming on the set of* Ruby's Relationship Rx. *Tempers flared. A vase was hurled. The cameraman landed in the hospital with a concussion. Not just any cameraman,* Liebchen. *Charles Begley Hutchinson IV, Hutch to his friends, the "Stud among Scuds" who was embedded with the 101ˢᵗ Airborne in Iraq. Who else but the Cowboy Cameraman is tough enough to join Team Ruby? You remember her, the drop-dead gorgeous Jilted Bride whose boyfriend put the kibosh on their lavish, all-expenses paid nuptials? She's baack, host of a new reality show that helps couples patch things up. Of all things. Only in New York, kids, only in New York.*

Scowling, Ruby snapped the paper shut and flung it into the nearest wastebasket. "Are they here?" She was referring to the show's guests, back again from yesterday, he of the wandering eye and she of the Mariano Rivera pitching arm.

Colin nodded. "In the greenroom. Made up and ready to go."

The couple had been persuaded to return following a phone call from the producer and the promise of serious swag from the show's sponsors.

Hutch lifted his head from his lens. "Get set for round two."

Ruby shot him a look to indicate she found his comment irritating. In fact, everything about the man was irritating. She pursed her lips. "Things will go much smoother today. We're finding our stride. You'll see."

Neither man replied. Ruby reviewed her notes while Colin fetched the guests and got them settled. She preferred not to speak to her guests before the camera rolled, so as not to dilute the power of her interactions. She checked her makeup once more in a small mirror she'd hung just outside of camera range. Her face was flawless, which always helped. She made her entrance. The girlfriend had chosen to sit in the easy chair, leaving her boyfriend by himself on the love seat.

As body language went, it was a bad sign.

"Welcome back," Ruby said brightly. "Let's roll."

The young woman fidgeted with the hem of her dress while her boyfriend stared at a spot on the wall.

Ruby cleared her throat and smiled at the camera. "Today, we pick up where we left off. Can this couple overcome one man's infidelity? Can they work together to stay together?

"I am your host, Ruby Lattingly, and that's the goal of my new show, *Ruby's Relationship Rx*. First, we identify the problem, and then we prescribe a solution." These words were the tagline of her show, and she punctuated them with her index finger. She had dreamed up the concept herself after the first show was canceled. That one, *Having It All,* was scrapped by the producers once Ruby's own wedding was called off, and she herself had gone from having it all to losing it all.

Hutch panned back now for a wide angle as Ruby flicked her hair over her shoulders, a move she knew from experience would show up well on film. She smiled. "When we left off yesterday, Alyssa and her boyfriend, José, had reached a turning point in their relationship. Let's review the issues."

José's forehead was covered in sweat despite the layer of talc Colin had applied. He cleared his throat noisily and began. "I wanted to take things to the next level, and I, uh, I . . ."

Ruby leaned in close, encouraging. "José, remember our goal. Working together to stay together."

"I wanted to make things more permanent between us," José said, wrenching his collar as though he was being choked. "And I figured it would be a good idea to run it past an old friend. You know, just for old times' sake."

Alyssa cut him off. "Old times' sake, my foot! You took your old girlfriend out for a romantic dinner!" Her knuckles went white, and she looked around, as though searching for something to fling.

Hutch flinched.

But Ruby had planned ahead, removing all knickknacks from the set. "This is good, very good," she said in a soothing tone.

Alyssa sniffed.

Her boyfriend continued to yank at his collar. "I wanted to take our relationship to the next step. I just needed to work it through first in my mind."

"Hah!" his girlfriend exclaimed.

"Remember," Ruby said, trying to get the show back on track, "our goal is to identify the problem and prescribe the solution. So, we're halfway there."

Alyssa glared. "Except that he waited till I was out of town. Then he invited his old girlfriend out to dinner." She stared at her boyfriend. "What were you thinking?"

Ruby's mind raced. As host, she was supposed to stay neutral. But it was hard not to take sides. "This is all good," she repeated in a soothing tone.

José's tone was pleading. "Alyssa, honey, please. I can explain. It was no big deal."

" 'No big deal'?" Alyssa was on her feet, jabbing a finger into the air. "You took her to *our* place, the restaurant where we always go. You sat with her at *our* favorite table."

"You did that?" Ruby stared at José, her soothing tone forgotten.

"They shared tiramisu for dessert. One plate, two forks!" Alyssa wailed. "That's *our* special thing!"

Ruby shook her head in agreement. "That's bad."

"See? I told you I'm right." Alyssa nodded vigorously.

Throwing his hands up in protest, José directed his next comments at Ruby. "You're siding with her. Aren't you supposed to stay neutral?"

Alyssa was already turning to go. "You are a no-good, lying, cheating, sneak of a man! And I wouldn't marry you if you were the last man on earth!"

"Now, wait a minute," Ruby began. But it was too late. Alyssa wrenched her microphone off as her boyfriend pleaded with her to stay. Ruby hesitated. This wasn't how it was supposed to happen. *Ruby's Relationship Rx* was supposed to help couples resolve their differences, not break up. But in all honesty, Alyssa would be much better off without José. Nobody needed a man who took his ex out to dinner, after all. And yet Ruby's show was going down in flames. "Now, Alyssa," Ruby called. "Let's spend some quality time on this, and figure out where we go from here."

The young woman shook her head. "No deal." She looked at her boyfriend. "It took coming onto this show for me to realize I'm better off without you."

Ruby couldn't suppress a nod of agreement.

"This is just wrong," her boyfriend protested.

But it was too late. Alyssa was heading out the door.

Her boyfriend followed.

Ruby stood, aware the camera was still recording, uncertain how to salvage this. She had drawn up lots of different scenarios for *Ruby's Relationship Rx,* but this wasn't one of them. Mustering her most professional smile, she faced the camera. "Sometimes things don't turn out exactly as we expect them to. And that is okay. *Ruby's Relationship Rx* is all about seeing what needs to be fixed and then fixing it."

She detected a low, hissing sound from Hutch but ignored it, signaling him to stop filming.

Hutch began breaking down his tripod.

Ruby stared at him, waiting. "So?"

"Guess that's a wrap," he said, not bothering to look up.

At least he didn't say, *I told you so.* Ruby looked to Colin for reassurance, but he was busy rolling up wires as fast as he could.

Ruby unhooked her cordless mike and smoothed her silk blouse, electric blue to match her eyes. "They probably weren't ready for the show's concept."

Hutch studied her, rolling his tongue inside his mouth from one cheek to the other, slowly and deliberately. He said nothing.

Ruby wasn't sure why she found this unsettling, but she did. She tried to say something to lighten the mood. "How do you say it in Texas? You can lead a horse to water, but you can't make it drink?"

Hutch's eyebrows rose slowly into his broad forehead as he considered this. "Yeah, that's what we say in Texas." He turned back to his tripod.

Colin had already donned his jacket and was headed for the door, makeup kit tucked under one arm. "See you, boss. Give me a shout when we're ready to roll again."

Colin was one of Ruby's best friends from way back, but he also worked on a per diem basis. Meaning he knew when to hit the road. Colin was nobody's fool.

Which left Ruby feeling very much alone.

Except for Hutch, who had finished stowing his gear and was now buttoning his jacket. "Well, I'll see you tomorrow. I'll be here at nine for the next victims—uh—couple."

Ruby gave a tight, closed-lipped smile. The last thing she needed was a sarcastic cameraman.

Especially when he was right.

"Don't worry. Things could still work out. Your show could become a reality hit like *Survivor*," said Colin. "You just need to fine-tune your strategy."

In addition to being Ruby's guy Friday, Colin's job description called for him to side with Ruby in everything. Something he was not doing with any real gusto at the moment. Ruby frowned. "What do you mean, fine-tune my strategy?"

Colin chose that moment to scoop up the last bite of his Madison tuna salad. He gestured helplessly at his full mouth.

Coward.

They were dining at Fred's on the ninth floor of Barney's, the Madison Avenue department store that always had a line of limos double-parked outside. Fred's was famous for the views, not outside but inside, where fashion glitterati competed for the best table each day, turning lunch into an extreme sport.

"What's wrong with my strategy?" Ruby repeated, taking a sip of her lemon ice water.

Colin put his fork down, considering his words before speaking. "Darling, you've been through a lot."

Ruby's eyes narrowed. She knew where this conversation was headed, and she didn't like it one bit. "Old ground."

"I know, Princess, but still."

Princess was his pet name for Ruby, and she loved it. Which was the only reason she tolerated him now for bringing up the not-distant-enough past.

"Look," Colin began gently, "you were terribly hurt when your fiancé canceled your wedding, and nobody can blame you for that. But, it just seems . . ." His voice faded.

Ruby spooned the last few drops of her low-fat chicken soup into her mouth and waited. "Seems like what?"

Colin reached for a hunk of semolina bread from the basket and made a production of swirling it around the plate of extra virgin olive oil that had been placed on the table for that purpose.

Neither of them would be caught dead wasting calories on a slab of semolina bread, even if had been baked fresh and trucked in from Astoria that very morning. He was stalling.

Ruby waited, calling his bluff.

Colin finally dropped the bread and plunged in. "Princess, the only thing in need of a total makeover around here is your attitude."

"What?" Ruby set her spoon down, hard.

"Sorry, but it's true. I know you don't want to hear this, but you haven't been the same since your wedding was called off. I can only imagine how painful it was, being thrown over at the last minute for another woman, not to mention the public humiliation."

Ruby winced. She wished everyone would forget about her broken engagement, or at least just stop talking about it. She'd had no idea what a mess she was getting into when she entered that stupid contest from *White Weddings* magazine. It had seemed so simple—write an essay to win a free wedding along with the services of Ethel Van Winterden, wedding planner to the stars. Ruby hadn't expected to win, any more than she had expected her fiancé to fall in love with Mrs. Van Winterden's assistant. Sighing, she closed her eyes to shut out the memory.

"You went through a lot," Colin continued in his soothing, best-pal tone of voice. "And your ex hurt you. But you can't take it out on every man who comes along."

The only reason she let Colin get away with saying

things like that was because he'd known her since she was a brunet. "I don't believe I'm taking anything out on every man who comes along," she said stiffly.

He cocked an eyebrow. "Then why did you make that poor guy confess to having one single, harmless little date with his ex-girlfriend? He said he only did it to remind himself how wrong she was for him."

"That's ridiculous," Ruby snapped. "No man should ever go out to dinner with another woman behind his girlfriend's back. Never."

Colin shrugged. "But he said he was only doing it for old times' sake. If he were really into her, he'd still be with her. It's simple."

Ruby stared, unbelieving. They all stuck together. All of them. Men. Even Colin. "That's ridiculous," Ruby said finally.

Colin gave her a knowing look. "All I'm saying is, you were hurt when your engagement was canceled. And I think it's possible that maybe, just maybe, you are taking it out on all men. But obviously, you weren't meant to marry your ex-boyfriend. Somewhere out there, the perfect man is waiting for you." He looked around the crowded dining room, as though Ruby's True Match might be dining at one of the nearby tables.

But when Ruby followed his gaze, she saw only the usual crowd. The Beautiful People. Retailers, fashion models, and even a famous diarist for the nation's top glossy magazine. All of the men were gay. Except for the writer. He was in his eighties.

Ruby sighed. Her True Match was nowhere in sight.

"It's time to put the past behind you," Colin said solemnly, "and dare to love again."

Love again? Was he kidding? Because he was starting to sound like one of the storyboards from her show. Ruby scowled. "I'm not afraid to fall in love again."

"Then why are you insisting on going date-free for an entire year?"

"I'm more concerned with my career right now. I want to make *Ruby's Relationship Rx* the runaway hit of reality television." It looked good on paper. But it sounded like a lame excuse, and Ruby knew it. She tried again. "Besides, I just haven't met anyone."

Colin rolled his eyes and arched his eyebrows, an impressive accomplishment for someone who took regular injections of Botox.

Ducking her head, Ruby dug through her pocketbook for lipstick.

"What about the Cowboy Cameraman?" Colin asked.

Ruby practically choked on her lip brush. "Hutch? You've got to be kidding."

Colin gave a sly smile. "I'd say 'the lady doth protest too much.' "

"Shakespeare is so played," Ruby murmured without looking up. She needed to nip this in the bud. Colin was like a dog with a bone once he got hold of an idea. "And, like everything else you've said today, it's ridiculous."

"Yummy!" came the reply.

There was no way of telling whether Colin was referring to Hutch or to the waiter who was passing with a tray of Fred's signature thin-crust pizzas.

"I suppose you could call him yummy," Ruby said, touching up her matte base. "If you go for that tall, macho, Texas type."

"So! You *do* have a thing for Hutch!"

Ruby snapped her compact shut. "I do not."

Colin gave a wicked giggle. "You do. I knew it all along. I can tell."

She shook her head so hard, her ponytail bounced around her long neck. "He's not my type. Sooo not my type, in fact, that he would not be my type if he were the last man on earth."

But the smug smile wasn't budging from Colin's face. Really, he could be annoying. Ruby rolled her eyes.

Colin reached for her hand, serious now. "Darling, you went through a terrible ordeal. Just awful."

Ruby winced.

"But don't you think it's time you jumped back into the pool?" He motioned with his free hand as if it were a flipper.

Ruby shook her head. "I'm over it. And I'm taking a year off to focus on my career. Dating someone like Hutch would be a mistake. For one thing, he's headed back to Iraq the first chance he gets. For another, I'm his boss."

Colin snorted. They both knew this meant nothing.

"But most of all"—Ruby leaned forward for emphasis—"he is Not. My. Type."

"Oo-kay," Colin said. "But I just don't see how you can give good advice on your show until you really and truly heal from the pain in your own past."

Pain in her own past? Maybe Colin should host a talk

show himself. Until then, the only pain around here was Colin. A fact Ruby would have pointed out if Colin hadn't checked his watch just then. He stood. "Sorry, Princess, I've got to go."

They'd spent the afternoon scouring Barney's lower floors for the perfect outfit for Colin's big date tonight.

"Time for my cucumber facial and no-polish manicure at the Salon on Seven."

Colin gave new meaning to the term *metrosexual.*

He pecked her on the cheek and was gone.

Everyone, it seemed, was dating someone. Except Ruby. She hadn't dated anyone since . . . Her mind was suddenly invaded by the image of the Vera Wang wedding gown she had chosen, all seventeen yards of moiré silk, including the train. Being tossed aside at the last minute had hurt. Even though she was glad she wasn't going to go through life with the wrong man, the thought of that Vera Wang gown and the seven bridesmaids' dresses in complementary shades of peach was still enough to make Ruby wince. She felt an old, familiar rumbling in her stomach that made her feel empty inside.

She pushed the memories away. She didn't need to start dating again to put the past to rest, she told herself stubbornly. She could do that very well solo, by way of her very own smash hit cable TV show.

She had landed the show, but at the moment it was off to a bad start.

Which no doubt accounted for the steady rumbling in her stomach. Darn. Ruby did not like tension of any kind. It was bad for the complexion.

The waiter came by with the check. As a formality, he offered dessert.

None of the fashionistas who ate at Fred's ever ordered dessert.

Ruby never ate dessert.

But the rumbling in her stomach persisted. "What have you got?" she asked.

The waiter looked pleasantly surprised. "Genuine *Ciao Bella* gelato. Just like in Italy."

Ice cream was Ruby's downfall.

"We've got a choice today of Verona chocolate or pistachio. Homemade."

Ruby couldn't help herself. "I'll have a scoop of each."

Chapter Five

Gilbert Beatty sat on the edge of a love seat on the set of *Ruby's Relationship Rx*, one corduroy pant leg crossed on top of the other, studying the laces of his suede Hush Puppies. He flecked at a tiny piece of lint on his corduroys, recrossed his legs, and swiped a hand through his hair for the tenth time.

The set was still except for Hutch, who adjusted the angle of his lens. The recording light was on.

There was a small sound from inside the covered birdcage on the cushion beside Gilbert, and he leaned over to murmur something soft and low into the folds of dark cloth that draped the cage.

From the easy chair at the end of the coffee table, Gilbert's girlfriend, Marsha, scowled from beneath her towering, sixties-style beehive hairdo. "See what I mean?"

She pointed at Gilbert, her voice shrill and plaintive. "He cares more about that stupid bird than he does me!"

There was a squawk from inside the cage.

"Shh!" Gilbert lifted his head and put one finger to his lips so that it almost touched his long, bony nose.

A nose that closely resembled a beak. Ruby felt her lips twitch as she bit back a smile. If ever there was a couple in need of a wardrobe makeover, this couple was it. The woman had awful hair and bad skin, and the man looked like the nerd behind the pink door from the board game Mystery Date. Ruby suppressed a shudder.

Hutch's head was buried behind the camera's viewfinder, but Ruby saw his shoulders shake with laughter.

"Shh! You know she doesn't like the sound of your voice!" Gilbert Beatty shot a glare at his girlfriend and kept one arm draped across the top of the cage.

"See what I mean?" the girlfriend shrieked again.

There was another loud squawk from inside the cage.

Gilbert leaned in close and murmured soothingly.

Ruby struggled for composure. She faced the camera. "Here we are, back for another edition of *Ruby's Relationship Rx,* where we identify the problem and prescribe a solution." She punctuated the tagline with an index finger. The movement caused her David Yurman bracelets to jangle.

There was another loud squawk.

"It's okay, sweetie," Gilbert whispered soothingly.

"This," Marsha hissed from her easy chair, "is the reason we need help."

"I'm your host, Ruby Lattingly," Ruby continued evenly. "And today we're working with Gilbert and his girlfriend, Marsha, who have a problem that many of our viewers might be facing at home." She made a sweeping motion with one arm to encompass Gilbert, who was hunched over his birdcage, as well as Marsha, perched alone in a wing chair. "Namely . . ." Ruby began.

"He cares more about that stupid bird than me!" Marsha shrieked.

Sounds of angry squawking filled the air.

"Would you please lower your voice?" Gilbert hissed, his small eyes blinking rapidly. "You know it upsets her."

Ruby was certain she heard snickering from behind the camera. She held up a hand, calling for silence on the set. "As I was saying, our challenge here today is how to integrate the relationship between a man, a woman, and a treasured pet."

As if on cue, the bird emitted another squawk.

Ruby smiled her brightest smile, signaling to the camera and viewers at home that this was one relationship problem that would be easy to fix.

Gilbert Beatty's girlfriend glowered.

These two deserved each other. Nobody else would have them. This was going to be a cinch, Ruby told herself. "Marsha, let's start with you."

Marsha sat bolt upright. "It's simple. He loves that bird more than he loves me. We've been dating a whole year, and he promised me that by now we'd be engaged." Marsha's voice broke, turning into a high-pitched squeak.

There were flapping noises from the cage.

Ruby gave Marsha a sympathetic nod before turning to Gilbert, who whispered something only the bird could hear. "And you, Gilbert? What are the issues you'd like to see resolved?" Ruby used her most encouraging tone of voice.

Gilbert lifted his head. "I care for you, Marsha," he began. "Deeply. More than any woman."

His girlfriend was weeping.

Ruby offered the box of tissues and waited.

"It's just, it's just that I . . . I mean, it's Tweetie here . . ." Gilbert glanced at the birdcage and swiped a hand through his hair again.

Like a bird preening. Ruby tried to push the thought away as she leaned forward. "We're here to help, Gilbert. Tell us your concerns for Tweetie."

"That stupid bird hates me!" Marsha burst out, her voice again rising to a high pitch.

The air exploded with squawks. The tiny cage shook.

"Now you've done it!" Gilbert shouted, tightening his grip. "You've really upset her!"

"Now, now," Ruby began. "Let's all take a deep breath and calm down. Let's remember we're here to work together to find a relationship prescription that works." Ruby gave an authoritative smile. This was her show, after all. She raised her arms wide in a gesture that was meant to be inclusive and expansive at the same time. Her bracelets jangled.

Which only intensified the squawking.

Gilbert glared at Ruby. "Tweetie doesn't like your bracelets."

Ruby's eyes widened.

Gilbert's tiny eyes narrowed. Like a sparrow's. "Take them off."

Ruby hesitated, not sure she'd heard right. "Excuse me?" She raised a hand uncertainly to her mouth. The movement caused her David Yurmans to jangle again.

"Tweetie doesn't like your bracelets," Gilbert repeated. "Take them off."

Ruby couldn't afford another breakup this early on into filming. So she slid her bracelets off, taking care not to make a sound.

"I don't believe this!" Marsha shrieked. "Now that bird is bossing you around too."

"Tweetie thanks you," Gilbert said solemnly.

"Tell Tweetie she's welcome," Ruby replied, feeling naked without her jewelry. "And now, in the interest of compromise, let's have Marsha take a seat next to you on the couch, and let's make some progress."

Gilbert gave a small shake of his head. "Tweetie won't like that."

"Our next step is to get the two of you together," Ruby said firmly.

The cage shook.

Marsha sat on the edge of the love seat.

Gilbert raked a hand through his hair again nervously.

"Go ahead," Ruby said in her most encouraging tone.

Marsha slid over next to the birdcage, which remained between the pair.

"Now take the cover off," Ruby directed.

Gilbert shook his head vehemently. "Tweetie won't like that."

"Don't be silly," Ruby said. "Tweetie just needs to get used to Marsha. She'll come to think of Marsha as a new friend, another person to play with." With no further ado, Ruby pulled the cover from the cage.

"No!" Gilbert and his girlfriend shouted in unison.

But it was too late. The damage was done. The cover caught on the cage's tiny door, which popped open, revealing a large, green macaw.

The bird sprang for it.

"Tweetie, no!" Gilbert Beatty cried.

The bird flew into the set's rafters, where she took a perch and glared down at them. Choosing her target.

"Don't do it, Tweetie!" Gilbert cried.

But it was too late. Tweetie made a beeline for Marsha's beehive.

Chapter Six

The waiting room at St. Clare's was deserted at midday. Ruby stared at the television, which was tuned to a soap opera with the volume switched off. Bored, she dug out her nail file and swiped at her silk tips even though they didn't need it.

Hutch dozed in the chair at her side.

Typical, she thought. Only a man could sleep at a time like this. Those chiseled cheekbones of his stood out in bas-relief; his dark lashes practically made their own shadows on his skin.

Ruby leaned in for a closer look.

Those lashes were wasted on a man. And the dimple in the center of that chin, apparently, didn't budge even when he wasn't smiling. And his big eyes, closed now, made him look boyish and surprisingly sweet. But there was something more, Ruby realized with a start. Charles Begley Hutchinson IV looked sexy even as he slept.

His eyelids sprang open as though he had heard her thoughts, and Ruby found herself staring straight into those hazel eyes.

He reached around with one arm and pulled her close beside him. Just like that, without missing a beat.

"Take a rest," he said in a voice that was low and husky with sleep. "You'll feel better."

Before she had time to protest, Ruby found herself nestled in the crook of Hutch's big arm, and, truth be told, it felt safe and good, just the right size. It had been a tiring day, and before she knew it, Ruby was drifting off to sleep, her nostrils full of the scent of Hutch—warm and musky—and her mind was full of him too.

She dreamed she was back in that windswept field again, under a sky so blue, her eyes hurt just to look at it. She wanted to swim in that sky, rise and rise until she became part of it, until the earth was a tiny speck down below, and the pattern of it, like the pattern of her life, would reveal itself to her from this great height.

Straining, she put forth a mighty effort until her ears were filled once more with the sound, delicate as baby's breath and just as fleeting. A soft, whispery sound like angels' wings. Ruby raised her face to the sky and was filled with longing. She wanted to rise up and become part of that sky.

She became aware of a warm, soft weight.

Someone whispered her name, low and deep, like a caress in her ear.

She took one last look at that sky and drew her breath in deeply, so she could hold that light inside her and feel its warmth in her core. She felt a fullness in her arms.

"Ruby." Her name again, whispered soft and low. She felt lips brush her ear. She snuggled in deeper to a cocoon that was warmer than anything she had ever known.

"Doc's here. He wants to talk to us."

Ruby's eyes fluttered open. She recognized Hutch's voice, close by. Her head rested on his shoulder, his face close to hers with his lips within striking distance of her earlobe. His cheek grazed hers as he pulled away, and she felt the scratch of his beard on her skin. It felt good. She breathed in deeply and took in Hutch's piney scent mixed with something else. Sage. Odd.

Ruby shook herself awake and blinked.

Dr. Hottie smiled at them from one of the molded plastic seats across the aisle. "Back again, Mr. and Mrs . . ."

"Hutchinson," Hutch replied, shaking Dr. Hottie's hand.

Ruby stifled a yawn, too tired to correct him. "I must have drifted off."

"That's okay. In fact, it's a good thing. She's been working too hard." Hutch placed one hand possessively at the base of Ruby's neck.

Ruby was about to shrug him off, but his hand felt good where it was. Besides, Dr. Hottie was busy flipping through his notes and didn't seem to notice.

Dr. Hottie glanced up. "The patient will be just fine. But based on the frequency of your visits, I think the two of you should find a safer place to work."

Hutch chuckled. "Tell that to the boss. She's about as stubborn as they come."

Ruby flashed him her chilliest diva look. "Maybe she just wants her show to succeed."

Hutch didn't flinch. "Maybe she should consider other people's point of view instead of forcing her own ideas onto everyone around her."

Ruby opened her mouth to argue but snapped it shut as painful memories came rushing back. Tweetie the macaw dive-bombing Marsha like a WWII flying ace, Marsha's high-pitched screams echoing off the walls, and Hutch racing to the rescue, sprinting across the set to pull the bird free from Marsha's beehive updo. And the tangle of arms, legs, and feathers that ensued . . .

Ruby winced. What if Hutch was right?

Dr. Hottie flipped his chart closed. "Mr. Beatty has a bad ankle sprain, nothing more. He's free to go. He needs to wear a bandage for a while and follow up with some physical therapy."

Relief flooded through Ruby. "That's great news. May we see him now?"

"Sorry, no can do." Dr. Hottie stood, signaling their time was up.

Ruby frowned. "Why not?"

"Ah, because, ah . . ." Dr. Hottie fidgeted with his beeper. "Um, there's no easy way to say this. Mr. Beatty never wants to see you again."

"What?" Ruby jumped to her feet so fast, she nearly fell out of her Jimmy Choos.

Hutch leapt to his feet and got his arm around her waist.

Dr. Hottie glanced at his beeper again. "That's probably the pain talking. I've gotta run. Nice seeing you both again." He flashed them a smile. "You tell that boss of yours to ease up."

"Will do," Hutch called after him.

Ruby could do without that last remark, thank you very much. But Hutch's arm felt good around her waist, as did the quick squeeze he gave her just then.

The way this day was going, she needed all the support she could get.

It was teeming rain outside. Ruby checked her Black-Berry for messages while Hutch set off in search of a cab.

There was just one message. From Leonard Klingston, her boss.

"Come to my office. Now."

Ruby shivered. Stray drops of rain blew in under the awning, spattering her blouse, which was Dry Clean Only, and making her feel even worse than she already did. The last thing she needed to top off this miserable day was a meeting with Klingston.

She folded her arms against the chill and scanned West Fifty-second Street impatiently. But it was raining, which meant all the cabs in New York had their OFF DUTY signs lit.

Hutch appeared at last, sporting a pair of small black umbrellas, the kind that were sold by vendors on every street corner in Manhattan the instant the sky clouded over.

"Umbrrrella, umbrrrella, umbrrrella," he trilled, rolling

his *r's* in a perfect imitation of the street vendors' sales jingle. He skidded to a stop, flourishing the umbrellas with a bow as though they were long-stemmed red roses. "Couldn't find a cab. Hope this'll do." His smile faded as he saw Ruby's face. "Hey, boss, I tried my best."

Ruby shook her head helplessly as hot tears pressed against the back of her eyes. "It's not that," she hiccupped, choking on a sob.

Dropping the umbrellas, Hutch leapt to her side and drew her close. "What's the matter, Ruby?"

Ruby's eyes welled with tears. "Klingston," was all she managed before a sob escaped.

Leonard Klingston was known in the business as the brassiest of network brass.

Hutch gathered her close, tipping her chin up gently toward his with one hand so she could read the expression in his eyes, which were full of sympathy. "Don't worry, Ruby, you'll do fine. He probably just wants to talk about . . ." His lips twitched as he searched for the right words.

"Tweetie," Ruby said, trying to sound solemn.

The word hung in the air between them.

"Tweetie," Hutch repeated.

Their eyes met, and they burst out laughing.

Ruby couldn't hold back. "He wants to discuss the avian incident."

Hutch threw his head back and let out a guffaw as if that was the funniest thing he'd ever heard.

Which it was.

Ruby laughed so hard, her eyes were now wet with

tears of a different sort than she had been feeling most of the day.

Hutch lowered his head, a gleam in his eye. "I guess you could say Tweetie ruffled a few feathers back there."

It was too much. Ruby doubled over, laughing so hard, she grabbed Hutch for support.

Hutch managed to hold her steady despite the fact that he was practically doubled over with mirth himself.

"Stupid bird," Ruby gasped.

That set Hutch off again, which made Ruby laugh even harder.

Until she caught sight of something that made the laughter die in her throat.

Gilbert Beatty, propped in his wheelchair, watching her.

"So, this is how you really feel," he said, his thin lips pressed together in a tight line.

"No," Ruby whispered in horror, raising a hand to protest. "That's not true."

"Oh really?" Gilbert inched his wheelchair closer as Ruby shrank back.

Hutch took a step forward, positioning himself between them. But Gilbert only sniffed, his beady eyes blinking with emotion.

He did look, well, birdlike.

"My girlfriend, Marsha, has broken up with me, thanks to you!" Gilbert motioned at the Ace bandage that was wrapped around his ankle. "And your cameraman inflicted pain and suffering on my foot. So all in all, I'd say coming onto your show was the biggest mistake of my life."

Ruby felt as if a grand piano had just landed on her

head from the top of the Empire State Building. Her ears were ringing. She opened her mouth to speak but couldn't think of anything to say.

Hutch spoke for her. "How's Tweetie?"

The mention of the bird set Ruby off again. Stifling a giggle, she pretended to cough instead.

Hutch gave her shoulder a quick squeeze as Gilbert drew in a deep breath and let it out in a rush. "Thankfully, Tweetie is okay. She's shaken but fine."

"Thank goodness," Ruby murmured.

"No harm, no fowl, I guess," Hutch said. "If you'll excuse the pun."

Ruby dug one of her Jimmy Choo heels into the top of Hutch's cowboy boot. Hard.

Hutch flinched but, to his credit, said nothing.

Gilbert Beatty's deep-set eyes narrowed to the size of tiny beads. "You haven't heard the end of this, Ms. Lattingly. I promise you that. I'm going to tell my story to the media."

His words hit Ruby with the force of a roller coaster that was starting its downward plunge. Correction, make that the granddaddy of them all—the Coney Island Cyclone, complete with the sound of all that wood clacking on the way down.

Hutch grabbed up the umbrellas, tightened his grip around her middle, and steered her away to safety.

They made their way down Seventh Avenue without saying anything. Ruby's mind churned. The media would have a field day with this, especially after the piece in today's *Post*. She had been hounded in the days after her wedding was called off. She winced. Her wedding, the one that had been touted by *White Weddings* magazine as *an affair to remember*, planned to perfection by Ethel Van Winterden, the founding editor who literally wrote the book on how to have the best possible wedding.

An affair to remember. Ruby cringed at the phrase. When her then-fiancé was caught, practically *en flagrante,* with the *White Weddings* reporter who had been assigned to cover their nuptials, the tabloids had put a new spin on the term *affair to remember.*

Ruby shuddered now, knowing all too well that when the press got hold of a story, they didn't let go. Not to mention the fact that the camera added ten pounds.

They sloshed through the rain. Ruby didn't even care that her favorite shoes were getting ruined. She waved off Hutch's offer of a piggyback ride. He fussed over her like a mother hen, steering her around the deep puddles, tilting the umbrellas to provide maximum coverage, using his body to shield her from the spray off the avenue.

"Cheer up, Ruby girl. This is like a walk in the park after some of the places I've been. And the scenery's as pretty as anything I've ever seen," Hutch said, flashing a big, easy smile her way.

Ruby managed a weak smile in return. Seventh Avenue with its boxy office buildings had never been her favorite. Plus it was raining cats and dogs. Plus Ruby had every reason to believe her show was about to be canceled. But Hutch had a reassuring presence, and somehow she didn't feel so bad with him by her side.

"That's better," Hutch said encouragingly. "Things will work out."

"Right," Ruby said tightly. She thought of Klingston The Barbarian sitting in his office right now high above the clouds. Waiting for her.

Her show was a failure, and she was about to be fired.

She was so lost in thought, she stepped off the curb before the light changed.

A horn blared as a delivery truck bore down on her.

Hutch swept her up into his arms and back onto the safety of the sidewalk. He didn't set her down right away, and for several instants she felt weightless in his arms, pressed against his heart. She felt his chest muscles working beneath his windbreaker.

His lips caught in her hair and lingered there. "Careful, Ruby, I don't want to lose you."

It was chauvinistic as heck, but Ruby wasn't complaining. She snuggled against him for one delicious instant. The light turned green, bringing her back to reality. "Hutch," she said in the strongest voice she could manage, which was not very. "The light?" She liked being sheltered from the storm, liked the way his arms felt around her, liked the way she fit inside them like a pair of fine Italian leather driving gloves. None of which changed the fact that she was about to join the ranks of the unemployed. She wriggled free and started walking. "Klingston's going to cancel my show—I just know it," she said glumly.

"Don't say that. Keep a positive attitude, Ruby girl," Hutch replied.

They reached another crosswalk with a large puddle. Without breaking stride or missing a beat, Hutch scooped her up, carried her across, and set her down on her high heels again.

A girl could get used to this, Ruby thought. "But Gilbert Beatty and his girlfriend just broke up, and that's one breakup too many for a show that's supposed to help couples stay together," Ruby observed sadly. She quickened her pace, anxious now to get this meeting over with. Hutch kept up easily, she noticed. Ruby wasn't used to men who were tall enough to match her stride.

Hutch was tall enough and then some.

He laughed. "The couple with the Tweetie bird needed to break up."

It was true. But Ruby couldn't believe she was on the same page with the Cowboy Cameraman. "You think so?"

"Yup." Hutch grabbed her hand as if to drive his point home.

Which made it hard to concentrate, but Ruby gave it her best shot. "I would have thought Marsha should cut him some slack. That's the 'Guy Point of View,' isn't it?"

"Nope." Hutch didn't even break stride.

"But I went out and hired an animal therapist to help Tweetie accept Marsha as the alpha bird."

Hutch threw his head back and laughed. "Don't tell me there's such a thing as an animal therapist in New York."

Three full pages in the *Yellow Book,* to be exact. "So, you think Gilbert was right to part ways with his girlfriend?"

Hutch grinned. "I think Gilbert should forget about dating for a while and get another bird."

Ruby's eyes widened. Bad enough that she couldn't help couples stay together on her show, but now she had the added problem of not being able to figure Hutch out. Which was maddening. So she stamped her foot, which only splashed more rainwater onto her soaked shoes. "Why don't you make up your mind? I would have thought the Guy Point of View would call for more tolerance on the part of his girlfriend."

Hutch shrugged. "The guy's a freak. And his bird has a bad attitude. That girl can do better."

True. But this was not the Guy Point of View she would have expected from the likes of Hutch. He kept changing his perspective, which was annoying. Really. Ruby shook her head. "I don't get it."

"Get what?"

You, Ruby almost said. She caught herself. This was not about Hutch, not one little bit. She was not interested in dating Hutch. She was not going to date anyone. Not for another six months. "The mysterious Guy Point of View," she said at last, trying not to sound miffed.

"Nothing mysterious about it," Hutch said with a grin. "If we're happy, we stay. If not, we find a way to cut ourselves cut loose. Simple."

"It's not simple," Ruby protested. She didn't want to admit even to herself how much she wanted to understand Hutch.

They reached the cable network's headquarters, a brown granite building dubbed The Cave that took up an entire block. Hutch paused, adjusting the umbrellas overhead so it was as if they were standing alone on a tiny island. He stood close enough that a musky whiff of his aftershave tickled her nose and she could feel his heat radiate from his body in waves.

Ruby shivered.

Everything grew still as the sights and sounds of midtown seemed to fade away around them.

"Don't have any regrets about the Tweetie breakup when you talk to Klingston," Hutch began.

At this distance, it was impossible not to hang onto his every word, so Ruby found herself doing just that.

The muscles in his jaw were working overtime, and Ruby sensed that Hutch had difficulty sharing his deepest feelings. But something told her he was about to do just that.

He cleared his throat. "If a man makes up his mind about a woman, that she's the one for him, then that's that."

Ruby was listening so hard, she felt herself start to sway. But Hutch had a hand steady at the small of her back, supporting her. She waited. And waited some more.

But Hutch said nothing.

"And so?"

Hutch smiled and gave a small shrug. "That's it."

"That's it? That's the Guy Point of View?"

He smiled as if he had just cracked the DNA code of some dreaded disease. "Yup. If we've made up our minds, we stay. If we're not ready, we go."

Ruby's eyes widened in disbelief. "So, it's that simple?"

He watched her face and saw that she was not convinced. He looked around, staring off into the distance as though the words he needed might be written on one of the electronic billboards that flashed day and night in nearby Times Square. Giving a small shrug, he took a deep breath in and let it out slowly before speaking. "When a man has made up his mind he's met the woman he wants to spend the rest of his life with, he's done. Nothing will get in his way. Nothing." Hutch had fixed those hazel eyes on hers with the intensity of a laser beam.

Ruby could hardly think straight. That laser beam was piercing her, melting the glacier that had formed around her heart. She forced herself to concentrate on what Hutch was saying, because she had the feeling that many women before her would have given up their right arms to hear him say these words. The theory of love, according to Charles Begley Hutchinson IV.

His eyes had a dreamy look of big space and open plains, the Faraway. "Once a man has met his match, he'll marry her. And he won't have any second thoughts."

Ruby was locked in his gaze, and she stood stock-still, wondering how many women had wandered into Hutch's Faraway and never found their way back. At the moment she was very glad she wasn't one of them.

"Well," Ruby said finally, trying to ignore the fluttering she felt in her heart. It was something she had never felt before, not even when she was engaged. That love had been tame, orderly, confined. This fluttering was anything but. It felt wild and huge, like the beating of wings climbing into an electric blue sky. Like doves on an open prairie. The sensation frightened her, and she took a step back. "I've gotta run."

He nodded. As if he had no doubts she would be back. "Go get 'em, Ruby."

The mighty soaring feeling did a quick fade when Ruby stepped off the elevator on the thirty-third floor. The network's policy of open-plan seating did not extend to the top executives who worked up here, she noticed. Klingston's office had real walls and a door, which at the moment was firmly shut.

"Go on in. He's waiting for you," the receptionist said without looking up.

Try as she might, Ruby lost the feel of those doves cooing to each other on the open plains. What she had was a sinking feeling, a squelching pair of ruined Jimmy Choos, and a faint rumbling in her stomach once more.

She opened the door and walked in.

Chapter Seven

Leonard Klingston sat in his sleek Aeron chair behind a desk of chrome and glass staring at a large plasma-screen TV that was mounted high on one wall. It was tuned to the cable network's round-the-clock news channel. Specifically a segment called "Watercooler Flap," a midday roundup of light local news and gossip.

Gilbert Beatty's image filled the screen. He was standing outside his apartment building, one of those ghastly postwar monstrosities of white brick, his voice shaking with outrage. Tweetie the macaw was perched on his shoulder.

"I wish I had never heard of *Ruby's Relationship Rx* or Ruby Lattingly," Gilbert Beatty said. "She couldn't pull off her own wedding, and now she's ruining everybody else's love life. Ruby Lattingly must be stopped!"

The screen flashed file footage from last spring of Ruby's being fitted for her wedding gown, all smiles, under the watchful gaze of Mrs. Ethel Van Winterden, wedding planner to the stars. Next came a shot of Ruby's onetime fiancé dashing down the steps of City Hall, his arm thrown around the new woman in his life. The Other Woman. They were smiling, even though it was pouring rain.

It was raining now.

And Ruby wasn't smiling.

Neither was Leonard Klingston, the producer.

He hit the clicker, and the screen went blank—thankfully. "Have a seat."

Ruby did as he directed.

The room was silent.

Finally she snuck a glance at Klingston.

He was staring at the copy of the *New York Post* that was on his desk, spread open to Page Six.

Ruby felt her stomach curl around an unseen fist. "I can explain." She regretted the words as soon as she said them. Rule number one for dealing with the boss: Don't grovel until it's absolutely necessary.

So she forced herself to wait in silence, staring miserably at the rain clouds that pressed against the windows, obscuring Klingston's view of the New Jersey palisades.

Klingston drained the last of his extra large soy latte and crushed the take-out container with one hand. He tossed the crumpled paper cup into his wastebasket, never taking his gaze from the Page Six column on his desk. The cup landed dead center without even hitting the rim.

He was known as The Barbarian for his willingness to take on risky new concepts in programming. But Ruby suspected there were other reasons as well.

Klingston looked up at last, regarding Ruby with eyes set low and deep beneath a thick shelf of a forehead. "You made the news."

The knot in Ruby's stomach tightened. "I don't think that coverage is fair. I mean, we're only a few episodes in, and we're bound to be on some sort of a learning curve, not to mention . . ."

Klingston held up one meaty hand, indicating she should stop.

Ruby bit her lip. Right. Rule number two for dealing with the boss: Don't babble.

"First things first. How is Hutch's head?"

Thick as ever. "Fine," Ruby replied quickly. "I made sure he received the proper medical attention."

"Good. We're lucky to have him. He's got real talent."

At least someone does.

The producer smiled, his first since the meeting began. "He's eager to return to the news division. As soon as his leg heals, he'll be on the first plane back to Iraq. He is the Cowboy Cameraman, after all."

It had a better ring to it than Jilted Bride, Ruby had to admit. "Right." The last thing she needed was to hear Klingston singing Hutch's praises. "It will be a shame to lose him, but in the meantime I'm making good use of his talents."

Like wrestling distraught couples to the ground.

"See to it that nobody on your set requires an ambulance for a while."

"Right," Ruby said meekly. As rebuffs went, this was mild. Klingston could have said a lot of other things. Such as, he would cancel her show if even one more couple broke up. It's what she would have said, if she were in his Doc Martens.

"I'm going to fine-tune my strategy. We'll get there," Ruby said brightly.

Klingston considered this, drawing his bushy eyebrows close together on that thick shelf of a forehead until they formed one single, unbroken line.

A monobrow.

"I have a thought," he said at last.

A Barbaric one, no doubt.

"Oh?" Ruby tried not to squirm.

"The network liked your original show concept, *Having it All.* You had landed the perfect man, the perfect job, the perfect rent-controlled apartment, and a big wedding. It was fun." He made a small gesture with his paws to punctuate the word *fun.* Then he paused.

Ruby braced herself. She knew what was coming.

"And then things fell apart."

Again, not fun. Ruby's stomach rumbled.

The Barbarian lifted his shoulders in a shrug. "Your wedding was called off, and the media saw a story in it. There was a third party involved."

Ruby winced. By "third party" he meant the Other Woman. Ruby's wedding was supposed to have been the social event of the year, planned to perfection by Ethel Van Winterden, wedding diva to the horsey set as well as founding editor of *White Weddings* magazine. A cover story was planned. Until Ruby's fiancé fell for the woman who had been assigned to write that cover story for *White Weddings.*

Mrs. Van Winterden's PR team had been feeding the tabloids tidbits for months, so they gobbled up the lurid details when the wedding was called off. Leonard Klingston & Company quickly pulled the plug on the contract for Ruby's show, *Having it All.*

Who wanted advice from a woman who had just lost it all?

The thought of her broken engagement, even now, months later, increased the rumbling in Ruby's stomach. She tried to cover the sound by tapping her still-damp Jimmy Choos against a shiny steel leg of The Barbarian's desk.

But Klingston didn't notice. He was too busy frowning at the newspaper on his desk. Finally that caterpillar monobrow broke in half again, and he glanced at Ruby. "You were in a tough spot. No two ways about it."

"Yes." *Memory lane, here we come.*

"You did what I would have done. Left town till things blew over."

Ruby had unplugged her cordless phone and taken to her bed, getting up only to accept Chinese takeout deliveries. After three days in an MSG fog, she showered, packed a bag, and caught the LIRR Cannonball out of Penn Station to her parents' weekend place in Bridgehampton. She hid out all spring and summer, returning to the city six months later with a savage tan and her game face. Armed with a plan to rise from the ashes.

"You came back to us with an idea for a new reality show, *Ruby's Relationship Rx.* We liked the concept. Find couples on the rocks like you were, and use your experience to help them work things out, stay together."

Except that so far it wasn't happening. Ruby nodded.

Klingston tapped the paper on his desk. "The press is interested."

Not in a good way. She didn't say that out loud, however. She wasn't about to make this easy for him. If he was going to put her on notice, he would have to do all the heavy lifting himself.

So his next words caught her off guard. "I've got your next couple lined up." He swiveled around to his credenza, collected a Plasticine folder, and slid it across the desk to her.

Ruby was so relieved, she went weak in the knees. He had chosen her next couple. Okay, he had taken a little control back, but once she had a success story under her belt, she'd reclaim the reins. She slid to the edge of her chair so her body language said, *Can do.* She smiled and took the folder. "Great."

"I want to see big things from you." Klingston swiveled his Aeron chair back around to his keyboard, signaling that the meeting was ended.

She hightailed it out of there. Once safely inside the elevator, she snuck a look inside the folder he had given her. What she saw made her stomach rumble like Mount Vesuvius.

Inside was the story of a young married couple with eighteen-month-old twins who were struggling to save their marriage. They were desperate for guidance.

The elevator landed with a thud. Ruby gulped. It was one thing to preside over the squabbling of a couple that was only dating. It was quite another to receive a plea for help from a couple whose marriage was in trouble. They had children.

The rain had stopped. Ruby barely noticed. She walked quickly up Seventh Avenue, hoping a long walk home across Central Park would clear her head. By the time she reached the cluster of sidewalk vendors at Columbus Circle, she knew there was only one way to stop the rumbling in her stomach.

She searched the sidewalk vendors till she found the one she wanted. And there it was, a bright blue cart with puffy white clouds on the sides. And big, fat, laughing cows.

Those cows were calling out to Ruby.

She got in line. When it was her turn, she ordered a vanilla ice cream bar dipped in fudge. Jumbo size.

Chapter Eight

They began work the next day with the couple Klingston had chosen, a fact Ruby kept to herself.

The pair became known on the set as the Golf Couple because of the wife's complaint that the sport was destroying their marriage.

Ruby did a happy dance in her head when she saw them settle themselves side by side on the couch. That was a good sign. She signaled Hutch to begin taping.

"Today we're checking in with a couple who says golf is coming between them. She says he plays all the time. He says golf is the only thing that relaxes him. Let's see if our relationship prescription can fix it."

Ruby gave the camera her most dazzling smile. "I'm your host, Ruby Lattingly, and that's the goal of my new show, *Ruby's Relationship Rx*. First, we identify the problem, and then we prescribe a solution. Let's check in with our guests today."

Hutch panned back to get a wide angle of the couple on the couch.

"We've got lots to work with, starting with Marissa, who says golf has become the 'other woman' in her marriage," Ruby said, noting Marissa's outfit, which consisted of a faded rugby shirt hanging low over misshapen stretch pants. Ruby stifled a shudder. "Right off the bat, I'm going to give Marissa the adventure of a lifetime. An after-hours shopping trip to Barney's with her own personal wardrobe consultant." She paused for dramatic effect.

Marissa gave a tentative smile. "Thanks. That sounds great."

Golf Husband shuffled his feet, shifting his position on the couch, trying to get comfortable.

"And to top things off," Ruby continued, "we've booked a haircut and highlights with Adolfo."

Golf Wife's smile did a slow fade.

Ruby tried to hide her surprise as she realized Golf Wife was not familiar with Adolfo's work. "Adolfo, as our viewers surely know, is known for his groundbreaking approach to dry cuts." She paused to let this fact sink in. "His salon is located just blocks from our studio here in midtown Manhattan."

Golf Wife brightened. "Gee."

"Don't mention it," Ruby crowed, turning to Golf Husband. "And how does that sound to you?"

He shrugged. "Okay, I guess. She looks good now, and I suppose she'd look good with a new haircut."

Nonplussed, Ruby beamed at the camera. "Not just any haircut. She will be styled by the man who invented the dry cut. Adolfo will cut Marissa's hair one strand at a time. The result is guaranteed to make any man forget his golf game." Ruby winked. "We're halfway there. First, we identify the problem, and then we prescribe a solution. That's our goal here on *Ruby's Relationship Rx*."

Golf Wife frowned. "Um, so that's it? A haircut?"

Ruby smiled like the Good Witch Glinda. "That's just the beginning. We've got something really special for you. Private Pilates classes. With an instructor who trained under Joseph Pilates himself."

Golf Wife glared. "Pilates classes?"

Her husband harrumphed. "What the heck is that?"

Ruby tried not to let her glance linger on Golf Wife's midsection. "Pilates classes are the secret weapon of the stars. Madonna swears Pilates got her abs back into pre-baby shape." She waited for a gush of gratitude.

But nothing came. The phrase *jaw dropping* was a good description for what was going on right now with Golf Wife's mouth, which hung open slightly, as though she was hoping this would help her find the right words to speak.

"Not that you don't look great right now," Ruby stammered.

But it was too late.

When Golf Wife found her voice, it carried an edge that hadn't been there before. "My husband spends every waking moment playing golf, including after work and on the weekends. Which leaves me home alone every day with twin toddlers. I came here to try to get my marriage straightened out. And you think some new clothes, a haircut, and a workout at the gym will fix it?"

"Well, that's just for starters," Ruby said brightly. "Once you feel perky on the outside, you'll feel perky on the inside, and everything will seem better and better every day."

Ruby thought she heard a groan from Hutch's direction.

Golf Couple stared at her in silence.

"And we could all stand to lose a few pounds," Ruby added, sensing she was losing ground.

Again it was too late.

Golf Wife shook her head.

Golf Husband sat up straight, so close to the edge of his seat, he almost fell off.

His body language was no longer good.

He glared at Ruby. "That has got to be the most superficial advice I've ever heard. Besides, it's also just, just . . . plain stupid."

There was silence as Ruby searched for something to say. She tried a different tack. "We all know that sometimes it's tempting to let ourselves go, but it's important to keep up appearances. Keep some spice in the relationship. For instance, I'll bet your husband would get a charge out of seeing you with a fresh new look, wouldn't he?" Ruby said, thinking of the many happy hours she and Colin spent at the makeup counters in Saks. "What I mean is, experimenting with the new spring colors can be fun and . . ." Her voice trailed off as Golf Husband guffawed.

Golf Wife shook her head as if she couldn't believe what she'd heard. "We've got eighteen-month-old twins. I'm lucky if I get to shower by the time he comes home from work!"

"And yet we can fix that," Ruby said, trying to sound bright even though she didn't know the first thing about taking care of a house, much less twins. "With a new look, you'll discover a whole new you. And your husband will forget all about his preoccupation with golf."

Ruby saw Hutch shaking his head from side to side as if he was watching the ball at a tennis match. Determined to ignore it, she smiled at the camera and mustered up her very best stage voice. "And this is what we do here at *Ruby's Relationship Rx.* First, we identify the problem. Then we prescribe a solution."

Golf Wife appeared to have heard enough. "You mean to tell me that you think a haircut is going to solve our marriage problems?"

"Plus Pilates classes and a makeover," Ruby pointed out.

Golf Wife stood. "This is the dumbest advice I've ever heard."

"Don't knock it till you've tried it," Ruby said firmly.

Golf Husband leapt to his feet. "I told you it was a bad idea to come onto this show." He reached for his wife's hand. "Let's get out of here."

"Wait!" Ruby couldn't believe this was happening. Her guests were about to walk off the set. Again. She reached out as if to stop them, but Golf Husband shrugged her hand off.

"We saw that guy on the news yesterday, the guy with the bird." Golf Husband shot his wife an I-told-you-so sort of glance.

"He says you ruined his relationship," Golf Wife said accusingly.

"I did nothing of the sort," Ruby said, trying not to sound defensive. "They didn't stick around long enough to try my approach."

"Neither will we. C'mon, sweetie. I told you this was a waste of time." Golf Husband checked his watch. "If we hurry, I can find a foursome, hit the green, and still be home before dark."

With that, they were gone.

Ruby stared after them, miserable.

Hutch switched the camera off. "At least these two didn't leave in separate cabs."

"Score one for us," Ruby said in a dull voice. She had expected to have a tough time counseling the couples that came onto her show. Resistance to change was to be expected. But this was turning out to be much tougher than she had thought. She let out a heavy sigh. "I don't get it. Who walks away from a cut and highlights with Adolfo?"

Hutch's eyebrows rose. "Hard to believe."

He was not being sincere. Ruby could tell. She looked at him, eyes narrowed. "Do you have any idea how long it takes to get an appointment with Adolfo? He's not taking on any new clients till Christmas."

Hutch let out a low whistle of mock awe. "And I'll just bet Christmas is the busy season for ol' Rudolph."

Ruby let her breath out in a huff. This time there was no

mistaking Hutch's sarcastic attitude. "His name is Adolfo, not Rudolph."

Hutch's lips twitched. "Sorry. Can you ever forgive me?"

Ignoring that question, Ruby shook her head in frustration. "And they walked out before we could begin our therapy."

"Just like the other two couples," Hutch observed cheerfully.

She didn't want to consider what Klingston would have to say about this. Never mind the fact that the Golf Couple had young babies at home. The thought made her shoulders sag.

Hutch was beside her in an instant. He gave her shoulder a friendly squeeze.

It felt good.

"Look on the bright side, Ruby. At least nobody threw anything at anyone this time."

That much was true. Ruby felt a ray of hope. And a peculiar sensation where Hutch's hand lingered, a warm weight that felt good on her shoulder. As though his hand belonged there, comfy cozy. Except it did not. Hutch was her employee, not a potential beau.

Ruby shrugged him off. "Well, I'm glad nothing landed on your head."

Hutch took his hand back and stood there grinning. "I'm glad too, boss."

The word *boss* sounded like a nickname when he said it. He was a tough employee to manage. Really.

Hutch rubbed one hand across his chiseled chin, considering things, gazing into her eyes, so close she could

make out small flecks of warm yellow mixed in with the hazel color.

Funny, you couldn't see those warm flecks from far away. They added depth, as when a painter mixed colors on a palette.

"Ever think maybe Golf Couple just needs some time together, just the two of them? Maybe a babysitter and a candlelight dinner without the kids would do it."

More Guy wisdom. "That's a simplistic solution," she replied evenly.

"Simplistic? Or just too simple for you?"

Hutch was challenging her. Again. Ruby drew herself up to her full height, which brought her just barely up to the tip of his nose. "Everyone knows how easily men become bored."

Hutch blinked, considering this. "I disagree. They're married. He's decided he wants to spend the rest of his life with her. Right now, they just need some quality time together, to remind them why they got married in the first place. What she needs to do, if you ask me, is take up golf."

Only a man would suggest that a woman take up golf. Luckily, Ruby thought, nobody had asked him. Nobody needed a bossy cameraman. "Nice idea," Ruby said. "But what Golf Wife needs, in my opinion, is some time out for herself. Time to be a girl. Get a makeover, get her nails done, do a little shopping. Once she looks better, she'll feel better."

Hutch stared, incredulous. "And you think that will make everything okay?"

"Natch," Ruby replied. She was caught off guard by Hutch's response.

He threw his head back and laughed. So hard his Adam's apple jumped all over his long, strong neck.

Ruby wasn't used to being laughed at. She glared at him until he was all laughed out, which took longer than it should have.

"I can't believe you think a man gives a darn whether his wife wears makeup or not," he said finally.

"Why wouldn't he?" The question was out before Ruby could stop herself. She didn't want to hear more of Hutch's Guy Point of View right now. Not really.

"Because a man doesn't marry a woman just because of the way she looks." Hutch's voice dropped a few notches so it was huskier than usual. "No matter how beautiful she is."

The way he was watching her now was unnerving. Ruby cleared her throat. "On the contrary, I think a woman needs to take care with her appearance," she said evenly.

Hutch leveled her with those laser-beam eyes. "A woman's true beauty is inside."

Ruby's own insides were suddenly shaky. She took a small step back. "But men sometimes change their minds. Perhaps they meet someone else, and then . . ." Her voice trailed off.

"Uh-uh." Hutch shook his head firmly. "No, they don't." He folded his arms across his chest, and it was probably the worst time to notice such a thing, but his biceps rippled.

A tiny twinge moved deep inside Ruby. She tried to ignore it, clearing her throat. "Men have a short attention span. They don't really want to settle down. A woman has to use all her feminine wiles to win him over. She has to stay glamorous to keep him."

Hutch blinked, considering this. He moved closer to her now, warmth radiating off his body like a big hug. He ran one hand across his jaw, and she could hear the soft, raspy sound of his whiskers, and the sound was so intimate, Ruby felt her cheeks heat up.

"I disagree," he said softly. "That's all wrong." He watched her so intently, she felt as if there were nobody else in the world. "If you really believe that, then you've been hanging around the wrong kind of man."

Implying he was the right sort of man. It was an arrogant statement. And probably the sexiest thing Ruby had ever heard. Her self-esteem, which had lain dormant since her broken engagement, had a growth spurt right there and then.

Hutch stood his ground and smiled. As if he knew he had just proved some sort of point.

Ruby wanted to give in, smile back at him like some teenager with a crush at a junior high dance. But then she'd have to date him. And she was still only six months into her year-long Man Diet. "I should think you of all people would know how easily men get bored," she said instead. She added the next for good measure. "After what happened at your place the other night, with your girlfriend showing up and all."

"So, that's it," he said, his tone chiding. "Ruby, you've got nothing to worry about. I told you, Kristal is not my girlfriend." He moved closer.

So close, it was hard for Ruby to breathe without taking

in his musky, male scent. She couldn't help herself. She drew in a deep gulp and held it till she felt light-headed. When she tried to speak, her voice came out whispery and girlish. Not what she intended. "That whole thing just proves my point. You have a short attention span when it comes to women."

Hutch's features relaxed into a slow, easy smile. He leaned forward until his face was just inches from hers, his voice turning huskier. "That's not true. If you got to know me, you'd know that for a fact. You'd get to know the real me."

It was spoken as a challenge.

Ruby wished she could think of something light and breezy to say to take the heat out of the moment. But her mind was crowded with the thought of what it might be like to know the real Hutch.

"There was never anything serious between me and Kristal. That's one thing. And for another, men don't lose interest and move on. They don't. Not when they really care about someone. You've gotta believe that, Ruby." Her name sounded soft, like a lullaby, when he said it in that Texas drawl.

She gazed up into his eyes, which had also gone soft. She felt herself sway just the tiniest bit, teetering in his direction.

He moved his hands lightning fast to her shoulders to steady her.

The backflips inside her were so strong, she was sure he could feel them through her sweater. The teetering grew worse. Before she knew it, she was practically in his arms. The thought occurred to her that the soldiers in Iraq probably felt right at home with Hutch in the heat of a battle, his being so big and solid and warm and all.

"Ruby, Ruby," Hutch murmured.

She couldn't help but notice that her name sounded even better when he said it twice.

In fact, she wouldn't mind hearing him say it a few more times.

"When a man falls for you, really and truly falls for you, nothing can ever make him fall out of love."

His words poured over her like warm syrup, and she felt herself practically melting into a puddle right there on the floor.

A small cough sounded close by.

Ruby straightened up, still shaky.

Colin coughed again. He snapped his cell phone shut. "Hate to interrupt."

Really, Colin was wicked. "You're not interrupting," Ruby said, brushing Hutch's hands away.

"We'll finish this another time," Hutch growled.

"Fine by me," Colin said merrily.

Thereby proving that all men stuck together, Ruby thought sourly. She considered firing them both on the spot. But Colin's next words stopped her in her tracks.

"The *New York Post* called. They want a comment."

"Comment on what?" Ruby asked wearily.

"Uh, the show," Colin said.

"What about the show?" But Ruby knew the answer.

Colin hesitated, looking down to where he traced an imaginary shape on the floor with the toe of one shoe.

Colin was nothing if not loyal, Ruby thought.

"They say the show is jinxed. Every couple who comes on the set breaks up, and . . ." Colin paused, trying to keep his tone light. "They're saying it looks as if Gotham's Jilted Bride has struck again."

Jilted Bride. The label had more sticking power than Krazy Glue, Ruby thought miserably. She had moved on. Why couldn't anyone see that? She was aware of Hutch watching her. Ready to scoop her up as if she were some frail hothouse flower.

But hothouse flowers bloomed just once and then died.

Ruby straightened her shoulders, put her chin up, and willed her voice to be strong. "Call the *Post* back," she said through gritted teeth. "Tell them I have no comment."

Chapter Nine

Ruby spent a restless night, replaying the day's events in her mind.

"You think a haircut will fix everything?" Golf Wife's voice, accusing and hurt, echoed in Ruby's ears.

She kept seeing the mournful look in Golf Husband's eyes as he told his wife he was sorry.

Ruby came to with a start. What if Gilbert Beatty was right? What if she was on a losing streak? The tabloids would never stop calling her the Jilted Bride.

She waited for dawn, listening to the traffic far below on York Avenue. And the not-so-faint rumbling in her stomach.

At last it was 6:00 A.M. A respectable time to get out of bed.

She showered, dressed, and left for work, stopping at a deli along the way to take care of the rumbling in her stomach. Bacon, egg, and cheese on a buttered roll with coffee on the side. All that and change back from a five. The Big Apple was the best place in the world to live.

She arrived at her tiny cubicle to find a copy of the morning's *Post* on her desk, open to Page Six:

Buckle your seat belts, kids; it's going to be a bumpy ride. Sources on the set of Ruby's Relationship Rx *tell us the Jilted Bride is still jinxed. Four shows in, and nobody's staying together. Some say they should move the show to Reno and call it* Quickie Divorce. *That would make life easier for her guests, no? As for us, we're still members of Team Ruby. She's a resourceful girl, and in New York anything can happen. So don your splash goggles, and be sure to tune in,* Liebchen. *This is one show that's fun to watch.*

Ruby stared at the paper as though it was something her parents' cat had dragged in from the yard. She wrinkled her nose and wished she had a shovel and latex gloves. Finally she grabbed a ruler and pushed the paper off the desk and into the trash. A sticky note fluttered off, covered in The Barbarian's heavy scrawl: *Stay on this. LK.*

Ruby considered this. "I intend to," she said at last to no one in particular. She tossed the note into the trash and dumped some of the contents of her in-box on top of it for good measure. Burying it.

Anybody who bet against *Ruby's Relationship Rx* would lose, she told herself.

Low self-esteem had never been Ruby's problem. Well, once only.

She sat down and bit into her egg sandwich, which was now lukewarm, and checked her watch. Seven-thirty.

Plenty late enough to call the mother of eighteen-month-old twins.

Golf Wife was curt when she heard Ruby's voice on the phone. Ruby took a deep breath and plunged in, listing all the reasons Golf Wife should come back onto the show to fight for her marriage. And, she did not add, save the show in the process.

In the end, Golf Wife agreed. "Why not? I have nothing to lose," the young wife said wearily.

Her words stayed in Ruby's mind after she dispatched Colin and Hutch to film the Golf Couple for a few days at their home in Maplewood, New Jersey.

Ruby spent the time writing copy and preparing storyboards to go with the segments they had already shot.

She took frequent snack breaks to manage the constant rumbling in her stomach.

By midmorning each day, Ruby had nibbled her way through the bunches of carrot sticks and celery stalks she had brought from home with tiny containers of low-fat ranch dressing.

By lunchtime pangs of hunger drove her outside, and she headed north to Columbus Circle, where those cows waited.

Ice cream was the only remedy for the rumbling in her stomach, a fact she remembered all too well from her teen years and summers spent at a camp in the Catskills for chubby kids.

By the end of the week, she felt ready to take another stab at saving the Golf Couple's marriage. She felt good. Strong. Resolute. She decided to celebrate with a chili dog, fully loaded.

Ruby woke up early Monday morning. Hutch and Colin were due back in the office today to review the footage they'd shot in New Jersey before filming another session of Golf Couple in the studio.

She stepped out of the shower, humming a happy tune as she reached for her favorite pair of Lilly Pulitzer Capri pants.

She pulled them on and found they no longer zipped all the way to the top.

She stopped humming and gave the zipper another tug. Nada. Ruby frowned. She examined the zipper. There was nothing wrong with it, so she gave it another tug. Harder this time. It edged up two notches and jammed.

The problem wasn't the zipper. It was her tummy. The darned zipper could not close around it.

Ruby stared at her reflection in the three-sided, full-length mirror, turning first one way and then another. All those trips to the vending carts had taken their toll. She'd spent the last six years carving out a model-thin figure, and in the six months since her wedding was canceled, it was gone.

Her tummy was sticking out. Way out. And she had sprouted hips. And thighs.

She had lost the slim profile she had been slaving over since college, the one that had morphed from duckling to swan, thanks to a steady diet of grilled chicken (skin off) and steamed vegetables flavored only with imitation, butter-flavored spray.

She felt a pang of guilt at the thought of the newly purchased container of Chunky Monkey ice cream that sat in her freezer even now, waiting for her to tear off the plastic seal and dig in.

She shook her head in disbelief. She tried on a different pair of pants and then a tailored skirt, all with the same result.

Exasperated, she pushed hangers aside and went deep into her walk-in closet. Deeper than ever. She shoved aside rows and rows of hangers till she reached the very back. There, buried in the darkest recesses of the custom-engineered closet, was what she sought. Like every other American woman, Ruby had set this item of clothing aside, saving it for use in cases of extreme, dire emergency.

Like now.

Gritting her teeth, she reached in and found them. Hanging neatly where she'd left them long ago.

Ruby's Fat Jeans.

She pulled them on and zipped. They fit like a glove. Of course they did. Grimacing, Ruby added a hot pink sweater of finely knit mohair and topped it off with an up-to-the-minute Chanel bouclé flower brooch in shades of mauve. She fastened the pin to her sweater and judged the effect. Decent. It would draw the eye up, away from her tummy. A useful trick of the fashion trade.

With a heavy sigh, she turned away from the mirror and headed for work. With any luck, nobody would notice.

Hutch's eyes lit up when he saw Ruby. He smiled wide from ear to ear.

More like a leer, actually.

"Did you do something different with your hair?" He swiveled his chair away from his workstation, editing forgotten, to get a better look.

"Nope." Ruby's hand went instinctively to her hair and smoothed it, even though it didn't need smoothing. Her thick blond hair rested like a mantle on her shoulders, framing her face like the way it always did. She took a seat beside him. "How's the editing?"

He ignored the question. "Something's changed. What is it?"

Ruby shrugged, wondering if he could hear the beating of her heart, which had picked up its pace. Not as fast as a jackrabbit. Not yet. But it was on its way. "I can't think of anything."

Hutch gave her an appraising look. Not in an obvious way, but still. Enough, combined with that big smile on his face, to remind her that he was a cameraman and therefore didn't miss much.

"Guess it's nothing," he said finally. "I'm away a few days and you look better than ever."

She tried to ignore the trill of pleasure that ran up her spine at hearing that, calling to mind instead the network's zero-tolerance policy regarding sexual harassment in the workplace. She was about to review it with Hutch when Colin walked in.

"Hey, guys." Colin stopped dead in his tracks and looked Ruby up and down, top to bottom. "Have I seen those jeans before?"

Now color did rise in Ruby's cheeks. "Yes," she said through clenched teeth. "I've had them for ages."

Colin's eyes narrowed. "Since college, as I recall."

Colin had a wicked streak. She shot him a look.

Hutch leaned all the way back in his desk chair and stretched his arms lazily over his head, allowing his gaze to drop down to Ruby's jeans. He took his time and grinned. "Colin noticed it too. Something's different."

Ruby decided her best option was to ignore the situation and move on. "Let's get started, shall we?"

"Anything you say, boss." Still grinning, Hutch turned back to his editing screen and hit the Play button. "Hours and hours of twins," he said cheerfully. "Eating mush, drinking from sippy cups, having their diapers changed, chasing the dog. And Mom chasing them, mostly."

"Great stuff," Colin added. "Golf Wife is practically a prisoner in her own home."

Ruby nodded. "Good. I mean, not good for her, but it will show up well on film."

Hutch chuckled. "Oh, It's fun to watch. Here, see for yourself." Dimming the lights, he reached out with one hand and slid Ruby's chair over to his in one smooth motion, so fast it was as if she hadn't gained any weight at all.

His proximity unnerved her; their knees were almost

touching. Almost. Not quite. Ruby chided herself. She needed to focus on the task at hand.

When Hutch turned his head in the darkened room, their faces were mere inches apart. "Can you see okay?" He adjusted the screen so it was easy to view.

All Ruby could think about was the fact that he was so close, she could make out the shadow of the hollow formed in his face by those cheekbones and that monster jaw of his. Not to mention that she could smell his aftershave—masculine and musky, not too sweet. She couldn't get enough of it.

Hutch swallowed, and Ruby watched his Adam's apple sink slowly down, then up, the full length of his strong, lean throat.

She swallowed also, aware of his gaze on her. She made a point of frowning at the tiny images on the screen in front of her, as though she was concentrating on work. But all she could think of was how those big hazel eyes of his had lingered on her. When Charles Begley Hutchinson IV looked at you, you felt looked at. Appreciated. Not to mention that his eyes crinkled ever so slightly around the edges. Smile lines.

He was smiling now. "Are you okay?"

As though he knew full well the effect he had on her.

The effect he wished he had on her, Ruby corrected herself. She swallowed again. "Fine," she replied, annoyed at how high-pitched and squeaky her voice sounded. Not the voice of a woman in charge. "Just fine," she repeated, motioning with one hand so her bracelets jangled. "Everything looks good."

"Glad you like it," Hutch said.

Images of Golf Wife flashed by, as she was transformed inside a tony East Fifty-seventh Street salon. Other scenes followed. Golf Wife shopping with the aid of a personal wardrobe consultant. Golf Wife getting a French manicure with silk tips. Golf Wife having her teeth whitened at the hands of a cosmetic dentist.

Hutch was good at his job, Ruby thought. She listed the scenes they would use on the show.

Hutch frowned. "Those are all scenes of Golf Wife's makeover."

Ruby nodded. "Precisely. I want to show her transformation."

"But you left out all the scenes of her chasing her kids around the house."

"Right," Ruby replied crisply.

He gave her a dubious look. "But the scenes at home show why she's stressed out, while he's off playing golf."

Ruby shrugged. "I suppose."

"Without those scenes, viewers won't understand why they need more time alone together."

He was a quick thinker for a cameraman, Ruby thought. Which, at the moment, was a real pain, because Ruby had her own agenda. She'd had a week to think things through, and she was more determined than ever to show everyone the simple steps a woman—even a busy, stressed-out woman like Golf Wife—could take to reinvent herself at any time in her life.

As Ruby was doing with her show.

Hutch dug a glossy brochure from his camera bag.

"Here's a schedule of golf lessons for beginners. We can sign Golf Wife up right away."

"Thanks." Ruby gave the brochure a quick glance before tapping the screen, which showed Golf Wife in sweats and sneakers. "But these images prove my point that all Golf Wife needs to put some spice back into her marriage is to take a little more care with her appearance."

"Yeah. And this brochure," Hutch said, touching the brochure and, Ruby couldn't help noticing, brushing her hand, "illustrates my point that all Golf Couple really needs is some quality alone time together."

He gave a superior sort of smile as though she, Ruby Lattingly, host of the show, had a lot to learn about relationships. His next words drove his point home. "That's how marriage works."

Ruby's eyes narrowed. She liked a challenge. "We'll see."

Chapter Ten

"What do you mean, you don't give a hoot how I look?" Golf Wife shrieked.

"Honey, don't get me wrong." Golf Husband shrugged. "Your new hairdo is nice. I liked the old one, and I like this one too."

The camera whirred. Golf Couple was back for their second session on-camera.

Golf Wife twisted her handkerchief first one way, then another. "I sat in a chair for hours. I got highlights, lowlights, and I don't know what else done to my hair. Not to mention these!" She held up her manicured hands and wiggled her silk tips so he could see them.

"They're nice." Golf Husband smiled and checked his watch in a way that made Ruby wonder if he was late for a tee time. Not good.

Ruby turned to the camera. "This is all good," she said soothingly.

The recording light shone a steady red.

"As you can see, we're into another episode of *Ruby's Relationship Rx,* where we identify the problem, prescribe a solution, and work things out."

"Do you have any idea just how hard it is to do Pilates?" Golf Wife burst out. "I feel like a pretzel!"

Her husband hung his head.

Ruby kept her smile bright, professional, signaling that this was All Good. "And today we revisit a couple who say golf is coming between them."

"It's ruining our marriage!" Golf Wife exclaimed.

"I agree we could use some help . . ." Golf Husband began.

Ruby cut him off. She had learned it was best to allow the couples to speak on-camera only in response to direct questions. "Let's judge the results of our wife's new head-to-toe makeover," Ruby said, smoothing her skirt. She'd bought some new things, knowing she couldn't hide out in her Fat Jeans forever. She'd scoured the racks of her favorite trendy boutiques on Madison but discovered that most of the cute stuff only came in the smallest sizes.

She had eventually made her way to Filene's Basement, elbowing her way through the sale racks, hoping she wouldn't run into anyone she knew. She'd found some decent bottoms that would have to do until she started her diet, which was going to be tough unless her stomach stopped its constant rumbling. She liked the new skirt she was wearing, at least. It was short and flouncy and reminiscent of Provence, while accentuating Ruby's new curves, which had been under construction since her breakup six months ago.

Hutch's eyes had lit up like a marquis for a rodeo championship when she walked onto the set today.

He was all business now, though, zooming in for a close-up of the couple on the couch.

"You're missing the point," Golf Husband grumbled. "That makeup, or makeover, or whatever you want to call it, is a waste of time."

Golf Wife's gaze narrowed. "You're just saying that because you didn't want to come back onto this show."

"You're right," her husband replied. "This is a complete waste of time. In fact . . ."

He reached for his microphone, and Ruby's stomach lurched. She could almost hear his words before he said them out loud.

He spread his hands helplessly, palms out, and looked sadly at his wife. "Sweetie, you are the great love of my life. I want to make you happy, but I just don't see how some new clothes will . . ."

Panic rose inside Ruby. She suspected she knew where this was going, and it wasn't pretty. Tomorrow's *Post* headline was practically printed already: *Jilted Bride Strikes Again.* Ruby searched wildly for something, anything, to say before Golf Husband uttered words he could never take back.

She was saved by a loud, piercing whistle.

A hush fell over the room.

Golf Husband snapped his mouth shut, surprised.

Hutch whistled again, loudly enough to stop a herd of stampeding cattle. Removing his fingers from his mouth, he switched the camera off. "Sorry, folks. We're having technical difficulties. Will you excuse us for a moment, please?" He grabbed Ruby by the arm and whisked her off the set and down the hall.

The greenroom was empty at this time of day, except for a tray of half-eaten fruit and bagels.

Ruby eyed the food. The rumbling in her stomach was louder than ever.

Hutch closed the door and leaned against it, folding his arms across his chest. He let out a sigh.

"What on earth do you think you're doing?" Ruby hissed.

"Saving your show," he replied calmly. "And their marriage."

"You have no right to interfere with my show. If I need your help, I'll ask for it." But the truth was, Ruby had been terrified that Golf Husband was about to utter the dreaded *D*-word. But she was not about to admit that to Hutch.

"Trust me. You need my help," Hutch replied smoothly. "If you're going to keep this couple together, you need to start thinking like a guy."

There it was again. The Guy Point of View. As though the world would spin a little more smoothly on its axis if every woman on the planet could just adopt and accept the exalted Guy Point of View. Ruby gave Hutch a baleful stare.

Everything about him, all six-feet four-inches from the top of his thick brown hair to his plaid collared sport shirt to his chinos and his no-nonsense brown lace-up shoes, screamed Guy.

But this was Ruby's show, not Hutch's. She was about to explain that to Hutch, but he wasn't paying her any mind.

In typical Guy fashion, he had sidled up to the buffet and was busy slathering cream cheese onto a bagel.

Ruby eyed the bagel. "Even if I wanted the Guy Point of View, I certainly wouldn't ask a man who walked out on his own wedding." It was a cheap shot, but she'd give anything to know what really happened to the bride who had been intended to begin each day of her married life by making her bed with that wedding band quilt.

Hutch said nothing and kept chewing. After a moment or two he swallowed. "I'll admit I've made mistakes when it comes to women. But it doesn't change the fact that Golf Husband is married. With two kids. And what he really needs right now is a reminder of why he fell in love with his wife in the first place. And that," Hutch said, licking his fingers one by one, "requires some alone time with her. That's all. Trust me."

If there had been a takeaway lesson from Ruby's breakup, it was this: Men were not to be trusted. Especially when they told you to trust them. That was exactly when you shouldn't trust them. "Hah," Ruby said. Not the most original response, but it got her point across.

Hutch stopped licking his fingers and frowned. "What makes you say that?"

It was a reasonable question, and one that Ruby had never been asked. When she thought about it, her ex-fiancé had never once asked her how she felt about anything. And here was Hutch, of all people, gobbling down bagels and hanging on her every word. Ruby was caught off guard. The snarky response she had been preparing came out all wrong. "Because just when you think you can trust them, they turn on you." To Ruby's horror, her voice broke. "The man you thought you could trust turns around and tells you, 'Sorry, I thought I was in love with you, but I'm not. I changed my mind.' And then you're left . . ." Her voice trailed off. "Well, then you're just left."

Ruby heard herself, and what she heard was the sound of a woman in pain. She was hurt, just hurt. All the pain she'd bottled up came bubbling to the surface then, burning her eyes like fire and closing her throat around that familiar, hot lump.

A sob tore loose.

In an instant Hutch had his arms around her, gathering her close so fast, she didn't have time to protest. "C'mon, Ruby, you'll be okay. You are okay."

His words were tender, his lips brushing softly through her hair and across her cheeks.

Which just made her hurt feelings bubble up even faster, demanding to be expressed. A tear escaped and rolled down her cheek, followed by another. And another. She tried to blink them back. Her shoulders shook with effort. But it was no use.

Hutch kissed her tears away. He threw his arms around her in a bear hug so tight, she could hardly breathe.

But it felt good.

"It's okay, Ruby girl, you got hurt. That's all. You can

move on. It won't happen again. We're not all bad." Hutch's voice was low and husky, his breath soft and warm on Ruby's ear.

He rocked her a tiny bit, murmuring words she had lost all hope of hearing from any man. "I know it's hard when you've been hurt, but you've got to roll with the punches, let go of the pain, and try again. You have to push yourself. You need to trust again. Guys aren't all bad, Ruby girl. But we're human. We make mistakes."

Ruby was crying so hard now, her tears left a wet spot on his sport shirt. She hoped it wasn't Dry Clean Only.

Hutch didn't seem to mind. He was busy stroking her hair. Not in a making out sort of way, more like a friend. It felt good. "Come on," he said. "You can turn things around. In your life and on your show. You're the boss, right?"

That was something Ruby could agree with. She nodded, brightening, and sniffed. She felt a thousand pounds lighter.

Hutch reached for a paper napkin from the buffet table and handed it to her.

She dabbed at her cheeks and blew her nose noisily. Checking her reflection in the mirror that hung over the buffet, she uttered a silent prayer of thanks to Max Factor for the invention of waterproof mascara. Her nose, however, looked like a vine-ripened tomato.

And despite this Hutch was smiling at her as if she had just been crowned Miss Beefsteak at some hokey county fair. "Okay?"

Ruby nodded. She felt like a prom queen. Normally,

she would have been mortified at blubbering like a big baby in front of someone. Especially if that someone was a man. Her ex-fiancé would have left the room, too embarrassed or too scared to stick around, as though Ruby's emotions were something that could destroy them both. And in the end it was *his* emotions that had done them in.

Not Hutch, though. He showed no signs of heading for the exit. With one arm firmly wrapped around Ruby's waist, he steered her closer to the buffet. "Have a grape," he said tenderly, feeding her so his fingers grazed her lips.

It really was romantic. And for once the rumbling in Ruby's stomach stopped.

Hutch watched her chew. "Men aren't any good at telling women what they want. But we're pretty easy to figure out." He was still holding her hand, which was nice. "All we really want is attention. That's all Golf Husband wants from his wife. He doesn't give a prairie dog's paw whether she has a new haircut or clothes from Barney's."

Prairie dog's paw? Did Hutch really just say that? Normally, Ruby would have thought of some snappy comeback to put him in his place. But she didn't feel like it. Truth be told, those hot, salty tears had melted the glacier inside her, the one that had earned her the nickname Midtown Diva around the set. She swallowed the rest of her grape and reached up to smooth her hair.

Hutch grinned. "You look great."

Ruby managed a shaky smile. "Thanks."

"Give it all you've got, Ruby girl."

As she turned to head back to the set, Hutch reached out and gave her a friendly swat on her behind.

Ruby practically jumped out of her Manolos. He was a difficult employee to manage. Really.

The rest of the taping went off without a hitch.

Ruby asked Golf Husband point-blank how he'd feel about some time alone with his wife, and he became as gentle as a lamb.

She wound up the show by offering them the services of a bona fide English nanny, a weekend away at a deluxe spa with tee times included, and golf lessons for Golf Wife.

By the time they were done, Golf Couple was giggling on the couch like a pair of teenagers in love.

Relief washed over Ruby from the top of her blond lowlights all the way down past her swingy skirt to her toes.

Golf Couple thanked her over and over again.

Ruby noticed that they stood arm in arm.

"At first I thought you were too prissy to give decent advice," Golf Husband confided.

His wife jabbed him with an elbow.

But Ruby was too relieved to care. She had helped them stay together. And lost about three tons of ice around her heart in the process.

Golf Husband pumped Ruby's hand. "Thank you for taking the time to see things from my point of view. I'm glad we came."

"Don't mention it," Ruby replied. "On *Ruby's Relationship Rx,* we have to be willing to take risks. And sometimes that means changing our approach midway through to get the results we want."

Hutch winked.

Good vibes were floating through the air like ether. So when Hutch invited Ruby to join him for a bite to eat, she said yes.

Even though it was four o'clock in the afternoon, and what hip, up-to-the-moment restaurant was even serving at that hour?

Chapter Eleven

Hutch kept Ruby in his sights. Nice view. There was harmony in the way the afternoon sunlight melded with the gold tones in her hair, which were repeated in her skin, which was flawless and creamy. Contrasted by smooth crimson lips that formed a dainty pout. And by her eyes, which were a crystal iridescent shade of blue, the color of a summer sky just before dawn.

The magic hour, as any photographer knew.

The camera loved her. He'd like to shoot stills of her. But, judging by the way she was evaluating the contents of her dinner dish, it would have to be for a vegan ad campaign.

Hutch grinned. "What's the matter?"

Ruby was seated across the table from him, wrinkling her nose at the thick slab of ribs that drooped over the sides of her plate, dripping barbecue sauce onto the plastic tablecloth.

Hutch laughed. "Just pick it up with your hands."

She breathed in through her nose, and her pouty red lips tightened.

Dang. She was cute.

She looked around the place as if she was she checking to see if she'd run into anybody she knew. But Harlem was well off the beaten track for the fashionistas she hung around with, which was exactly why Hutch had chosen Sylvia's.

That, plus he was hooked on Sylvia's world-famous barbecued ribs.

Using the tip of her knife, Ruby pried off a slab of rib and popped it into her mouth.

The expression that washed over her face was like seeing the sunrise after a long night. It proved Ruby had a soft inside despite her tough outer shell. Which was fine by Hutch. He liked clams, toasted marshmallows, coconuts, and pretty much anything else that was tough on the outside but soft in the middle.

Ruby was something, all right. She really was. He spooned a serving of okra and tomato gumbo onto her plate. "Try that. A decent meal will do you good. Now you know how we eat in Texas."

"There's probably enough trans fat on this plate to clog every artery in the city," Ruby said, glancing outside, where, as if to prove her point, the rush-hour traffic on Lenox Avenue had slowed to a crawl. She glanced at him and softened. "But these are the best ribs I've ever had."

Hutch grinned. "Probably the only ribs you've ever had."

She smiled and said nothing, so he knew it was true.

"You New Yorkers don't know how to eat," he teased.

"I beg to differ," she said, nibbling her way along the length of a rib. "We've got it all. A walk through the Time Warner Center proves it."

Hutch shook his head and grinned. "I'm not talking about two-hundred-dollar sushi or a seventy-dollar pizza with duck liver on top."

"Don't knock it till you've tried it," Ruby said between bites. She was getting down to business on her third rib; the first two were already picked clean.

A person couldn't be happy when all they ate was rabbit food. Judging by the way Ruby was going at it, she was one happy woman at the moment. Score one for the Regular Guy, Hutch thought.

Ruby's head popped up as though she could read his mind. "What?"

She was bright too. In fact, Ruby Lattingly was way smarter than any of the women he'd dated. Not to mention that the pretty way she used her napkin to dab at her mouth left Hutch at a loss for words. So he merely shrugged, content to sit there grinning like an idiot.

Charles Begley Hutchinson IV was smitten.

"Come on, you can tell me." She leaned forward, flicking that blonde mane over one shoulder so her bracelets jangled, dipping her chin, and smiling just enough to make him wish he had his camera handy.

Hutch couldn't help but smile back. He knew the signs. Heck, he had practically invented them. She was flirting with him. Ruby Lattingly, the Midtown Diva who reveled in the fact that she was his boss, was flirting with him.

Life was good.

He kept his high beams on, grinning like the Cheshire cat, taking his time. He shrugged. "Nothing."

She giggled. "What do you mean, nothing?" Leaning in another fraction of an inch, she gathered a few strands of her hair and began twirling it slowly around one finger like golden silk.

"You look good with your hair down," he said. "You should wear it down more often."

A flush came to her cheeks.

Ruby was no easy blusher, which made it that much sweeter. Hutch leaned back, enjoying the victory. He felt his jaw relax as a warm feeling spread slowly through him. He raised his glass of iced tea. "I propose a toast."

Smiling, Ruby raised her glass. "What are we toasting?"

"You." Hutch clinked her glass. "You really pulled it out of the hopper today, Ruby girl."

For once she didn't tell him to stop calling her Ruby girl. She sipped her iced tea instead. "Thanks."

Hutch sat quietly, mellowing out on the soft cloud of Ruby's flowery perfume, which trumped even the tangy molasses aroma of Sylvia's world-famous ribs. He leaned forward, closer to that delicate, heart-shaped face, close enough that he could see a pale sprinkling of freckles on that tiny upturned nose. "You're a star. You turned things around for the Golf Couple. That took serious effort. I'm proud of you."

"You mean, I finally got the hang of the Guy Point of View?" Her tone was teasing, but he could tell she was happy.

She'd be fun to take dancing. Hutch knew a place in Brooklyn where they did line dancing on Saturday nights. "Pretty much. You won first place in the Guy Point of View contest." He allowed his voice to drop a notch. "Want to know what the winner gets?"

She giggled, and he watched her cheeks darken with a flush.

Sweet.

"I couldn't have done it without your help," she said honestly.

"Sure, you could," Hutch pointed out.

She didn't look convinced.

"There's more to life than trying to look good. Don't get me wrong—you look great," he added quickly. "Just keep considering things from the man's perspective too. Once you get the hang of it, you won't even need me around."

But he hoped to *be* around.

Ruby met his gaze and held it. "I might keep you around," she said, smiling sweetly. "Maybe."

Something caved inside him like a tectonic plate shifting and crumbling at the edges, and Hutch had a pretty good idea it was his independence. Because this woman was able to twirl him around that little finger of hers the same way she was working her hair right now. In that instant Hutch knew his number was up. He sat back and enjoyed the ride. "It's not your fault you want to make everyone beautiful," he said with a grin. "You can't help it, Ruby girl. You were born that way yourself."

"Thanks for not holding it against me." She laughed, a sound that tinkled like a small bell ringing.

The melody of it made Hutch swell with pride. Ruby didn't laugh easily. She was digging this.

"Don't you give it another thought, Ruby. If you get off track, I'll let you know."

"That's good. Because we have some challenging episodes lined up."

Uh-oh, she was back on the work thing. Not good. "You can count on me," he said, scooping a bit of fried catfish onto his fork. "Here, try some of this."

"What is it?" But she parted those crimson lips without waiting for an answer.

Hutch felt his heart swell. "It's the sweetest fish you'll ever taste," he said, gently depositing a forkful.

Ruby Lattingly was eating out of his hand. Life was good. Hutch watched the rapt expression on her face that was a perfect match for the feeling in his gut. "If you like that, there's plenty more."

She swallowed, fluttering those dark lashes. She batted her eyes at him.

Hutch was smiling so widely, he thought his jaw might break in two. He let out a sigh of pure contentment. The weekend was off to a flying start.

"So," she said sweetly, "tell me about yourself."

Uh-oh. "What do you want to know?"

"For starters, how did you learn to take such beautiful pictures? Did you go to NYU film school?"

She was a real New Yorker, all right. "Nope. Rice University." It was one of the top-rated schools in Houston. "I got a degree in philosophy. Never took a camera course there." He smiled. "I'm self-taught in photography."

Ruby considered this. "I never met anyone who earned a living based on talent, not formal training."

She had probably never spoken with a cameraman before, Hutch could have pointed out. But things were going well. Why ruin a good thing?

"So, how did you become interested in photography?"

Hutch was about to give her his standard answer but checked himself. This was Ruby, and she wasn't like any of the other women he'd dated. So he told her the truth. "I got sick when I was a kid. Scarlet fever."

She frowned. "That must have been awful."

He thought about it. "It was tough on my parents, I guess," he conceded. "I was just a kid. I remember having to stay in bed for weeks. They set up a couch for me in the dining room so the nanny could keep an eye on me. The fever gave me a new way of seeing things, I guess, like how the light from the sun looked when it bounced off this big crystal chandelier we had."

Ruby perked up. "Nanny?"

He chuckled. "Oh, I get it. Nobody from west Texas would have had a nanny?"

Ruby's lips twitched. "Not even a big crystal chandelier, if you want to know the truth."

"It was a tight fit, but we squeezed it into the trailer," Hutch teased.

"Okay, okay, I apologize," she said.

"Apology accepted." He could tell by the look on her face that she meant it. He knew she'd love everything about his childhood home, from the wrought iron gates to the long drive lined with ancient oaks to the towering

Georgian Colonial at the end of it. She'd fit in with his mother and seven sisters like peas in a pod. But if she went there, she'd uncover the secret Hutch wanted to forget. And she would never forgive him once she learned the truth. Never. It was the reason Hutch didn't bring girls home to Texas. It was his cardinal rule.

And what a woman didn't know couldn't hurt her.

"Go on," Ruby said.

"I figured out that when I closed one eye and squinted with the other, I saw everything in terms of light and shadow. I could see how things would look in a photograph. It was as though a switch had been flipped in my brain. Nothing was the same after that." Hutch took in a deep breath and let it out. He wasn't used to talking about himself.

She watched him with a soft quality to her expression he hadn't seen before. Her eyes said it all. They were dewy, wide.

"Thanks," she said simply. "You have a rare talent. I'm glad you got a break from the news division to be with us for a while."

Hutch nodded. Neither of them mentioned that it was a temporary arrangement. Fact was, if Hutch had to choose at that very moment to go back to Iraq or stay in New York City, he was not at all sure how he would choose.

Ruby opened her mouth to speak, and he was afraid she'd ask him something stupid, like other girls did, such as whether he would ever settle down. "You know," she said in a voice that wouldn't melt butter, "I'd like some more of that catfish. It's the best I've ever had."

Ruby was one cool customer.

Hutch practically had to bite his tongue to keep from telling her so, through the rest of dinner and straight through the sweet-potato pie for dessert, till the cab ride home when he kissed her. Long and languorous and sweet, till he felt her body relax a bit and she nestled beside him, and Hutch didn't move his arm one inch during the entire drive south on the FDR Drive.

The taste of her stayed with Hutch, lingering like the soft, flowery scent of her skin, staying with him so he couldn't stop smiling all night, even in his sleep.

Chapter Twelve

"It was no big deal." Lie. Ruby tried covering her smile with a big sip of tea but couldn't pull it off. She set her cup down so hard that China black spilled all over the saucer.

Colin waggled a finger at her. "Princess? Come clean. I know that look. I've seen it before."

"I told you. We went to dinner, ate some ribs, talked about work, and went home. End of story. Nothing happened." But Ruby couldn't hold back a giggle. The thumping of techno music before noon might not appeal to most people, but it suited her mood on this Saturday morning.

Eyes widening, Colin clapped his hands with glee. "You kissed him."

"Did not." But Ruby knew her face was a dead giveaway.

"Did so, did so, did so," was the response.

Ruby tried to look dignified.

Ignoring her, Colin raised his glass of iced Sri Lanka spiced blend in a toast. "It's about time."

They were at the Tavalon Tea Bar downtown, known for its hip DJ and tea sommelier on staff. Not to mention pastries from nearby Balthazar.

Ruby gave a small sigh of surrender. Why keep secrets from a friend who had known her since the days of Jordache jeans? Besides, she was so happy, she wanted to say his name out loud. "Don't tell anyone on the set about my dinner with Hutch."

Colin leaned forward and waggled his hands near his ears. "First, I need to know what there is to tell."

"There is nothing to tell."

"Come on, you can tell me. I'm a doctor."

Ruby couldn't help but smile at their old joke. "Colin, I don't want to be the subject of gossip."

"This isn't gossip—this is me. Anyhow, everyone would be happy for you. You know, 'back in the saddle again.' And Hutch *is* the Cowboy Cameraman. Get it?" Colin watched happily to see if Ruby got the pun.

She rolled her eyes. "Take it easy."

"You know my lips are sealed." He raised a hand to his lips and made a show of turning an imaginary key. "Now, dish. Because it's about time you had some fun. And Hutch is the perfect man for the job. Honey, he is smokin' hot."

Ruby couldn't help but laugh. It hadn't taken Colin longer than a New York minute to go from mocking Hutch for being an alpha male to proclaiming him hot. Just like Ruby. Last night at Sylvia's she had begun to see Hutch for what he was: a decent, honest, Regular Guy.

Which made him as rare in Manhattan as a seat on a crosstown bus during rush hour. "Dinner went very well," was all she said.

Colin was merrily stirring more Turbinado sugar into his tea. "Forget dinner. Tell me what happened after."

Ruby bit into her green-tea cupcake, which was delicious. How could she describe her feelings? How could anyone understand? Hutch had been a strong, steady presence on the set for Ruby these last few weeks, proving that compassion did not equal weakness.

In fact, just the opposite.

Which came as a major 411 flash to Ruby, who had spent her whole life building a protective shell around herself.

So last night, when Hutch shared how he came by his unique perception of light and shadow, it banished some of Ruby's own inner defenses. Hutch had given her a glimpse of his Faraway.

He, in turn, had seen hers. And he wasn't running scared. There were simply no words to describe that.

"Dinner was good," Ruby said finally.

Colin stopped chewing his cheese Danish and frowned. "That's it?"

"That's it. I had a wonderful time," she said simply.

Colin's eyes widened. "You've fallen harder than I thought."

"I have not," Ruby protested. "It's just that it's hard to describe. You know that feeling you get when . . ." Her voice trailed off. She couldn't think of an example.

"Uh-oh," Colin said in a low voice. "You really are

done for. I've never seen you like this. Not even when you were engaged."

Even as she opened her mouth to protest, Ruby knew that Colin was telling the truth. "I don't want to make a big deal out of this."

"Too late, Princess, I think this is a big deal already," Colin said cheerfully. "I think it is for him too. I can tell by the way he looks at you. I've seen it for weeks."

Hutch was falling for her. Colin said so, and Colin was never wrong about such things. The realization thrilled Ruby, ratcheting up the zingy feeling she'd had since last night when Hutch kissed her. The memory of his lips on hers, surprisingly tender, made the zingy feeling grow. Ruby felt as if there were a thousand electric sparks firing inside her. "Let's not get carried away, Colin."

"Whatever you say, Princess. But I think we both know the signs." Colin gave a pointed glance down at Ruby's plate, where Ruby was busy shredding the remains of her green-tea cupcake into tiny crumbs and forming a pyramid.

It was an old habit, something she did only when she was happy. When her stomach didn't demand every last morsel of food on her plate. Because the rumbling had gone away.

Ruby felt so giddy, she thought she might just float away. It was too much. "Next subject. Please," Ruby pleaded, signaling for the bill. She wasn't ready to dissect her new feelings for Hutch, doing a postmortem on every date the next day with Colin the way she usually did. This felt different. Hutch was different. And Ruby was afraid it wouldn't turn out to be real. She suspected that the way she'd felt after her engagement was called off was nothing compared with how she would feel if she gave her heart to Hutch and he didn't keep it. If it came back, it would be shattered into a million pieces that couldn't be put together again. À la Humpty Dumpty.

Colin was staring down at the pyramid of crumbs on Ruby's plate as though he had a lot more to say on the subject, but he changed his mind. "Done."

Colin had his good points.

"What's the latest at work?" he asked.

"Good news," she said, signing the check. "Klingston found us our next couple, and we're going to try a new approach. Film them in action."

Colin took another gulp of his iced tea. "Do tell."

"We'll follow them around, going about their routine. Klingston tells me they're excited about coming onto the show."

"Guess they weren't watching the news last week when Birdman called you a threat to lovers everywhere," Colin remarked.

Ruby fixed him with an I'm-still-your-boss stare.

He shrank back. "Sorry, that was uncalled for. And you did save Golf Couple."

With Hutch's help, a fact Ruby didn't point out. But she felt certain she could turn things around now and really help the couples that came onto *Ruby's Relationship Rx.* Ruby had a secret weapon. Hutch. He was the expert in the Guy Point of View.

She knew she could count on him to help with this next

couple. He had given her his promise. And a man like Hutch always kept his word. "They're engaged and have some issues to resolve before they walk up the aisle."

Colin gave her a suspicious look. "What issues?"

Ruby was careful to keep her tone light, airy. "Oh, the groom has a small case of cold feet. And the bride has gotten a tad carried away with the wedding plans."

Colin's frown deepened. "How carried away?"

"Just your basic carried away," she replied carefully.

"Trouble-choosing-a-veil carried away or Star Jones carried away?"

It was a sore subject between them. Ruby's ex-fiancé had been all wrong for her. She knew that. But the fact remained, she had gone over the top with her wedding plans. Okay, more than over the top. Way into the strato-sphere. Which had nothing to do with her breakup. But, still, a low-key reception was not exactly Ruby's strong suit. Which was bound to make this next episode a real challenge. Ruby sighed. "They're in bad shape," she ad-mitted. "They overspent on the ring. She dyed the brides-maid shoes three times over and still isn't happy. The *peau de soie* is practically falling apart."

"What color?"

"Peach."

Colin groaned.

That had been Ruby's choice for bridesmaid gowns. "It gets worse," she continued. "They've rented out the entire Stuyvesant Club, and she's fighting over the menu with Pierre Doumouchelles."

Fear widened Colin's eyes until white showed around

the edges. "How many Michelin stars does Pierre Doumouchelles have now?"

"Two, maybe three." Ruby's voice was barely above a whisper.

Colin nodded in reverence. "Well," he said at last, "if there's a woman in New York who can hold her own with an angry French chef, it's you, darling."

A reference to the fact that Ruby had booked Pierre Doumouchelles back when he held just one star, to cater her own over-the-top wedding extravaganza. "Colin, I can handle this."

Colin said nothing and pursed his lips in an if-you-say-so sort of way.

The fact was, Wikipedia referenced Ruby Lattingly in its definition of *Bridezilla.*

Judging by the look on Colin's face now, even her best friend didn't believe Ruby could help another bride rein in her wedding arrangements.

"I can do this," Ruby vowed in what she hoped was her best leadership voice. What she didn't add was that she'd need to rely on Hutch for help. "We can do this—you, me, and the entire staff of *Ruby's Relationship Rx.*"

"Of course we can," Colin echoed. But his voice was hollow.

"And do you want to know the best part?"

The look on his face said Colin didn't think there would be a best part, but he took the bait anyway. "Name it," he said helpfully.

"This next couple is born to be on TV," Ruby said

brightly. "He's made of money—started his own hedge fund in Greenwich. He grew up in Bedford."

Colin brightened. "Maybe he can introduce us to his rich prep school friends."

Ruby ignored that and went on. "The lucky bride-to-be is from down South, so she's got that accent thing going on. And she's model thin. She'll be great on-camera."

"Fantastic." Colin lifted his glass in a toast. "Here's to a hit show."

They clinked. Things would work out. Ruby was on a learning curve, but she had a secret weapon, and his name was Hutch.

They prepared to leave.

Colin gathered his man purse. "Where's the bride from, anyway?"

Ruby blotted her lips with a napkin before applying a new layer of lip gloss. "It was on the application, but I can't remember. Flyover territory." *Flyover territory* was New Yorker shorthand for all the land between the Hudson River and LA. "Who cares? Somewhere down South." She closed her Birkin bag and stood, ready to leave. "Texas, I think."

Chapter Thirteen

Ruby surveyed the ballroom of the stalwart Stuyvesant Club on Fifth Avenue. The place had too much history. She tried to stay calm.

The big room buzzed with activity.

A team of sous-chefs fussed over silver platters under the menacing gaze of Pierre Doumouchelles, who stood tall in his chef whites and toque. A food stylist frantically fanned the Alaskan king crab legs with mousseline, complaining to everyone within earshot that the dish was starting to sweat.

Florists swarmed the linen-clad tables like ants at a picnic, putting final touches on centerpieces of red roses mixed with rare orchids, illuminated by the twinkling light of hand-dipped candles made of wax from bees that had been raised on a diet of organically farmed flowers.

Buffet tables along the walls were loaded down with

camera-ready samples of everything required for an over-the-top wedding reception, from engraved linen stationery to champagne chilling in silver buckets of ice. There were enough Spode place settings to feed a platoon, with silver cutlery and handblown crystal stemware to match.

In short, everything required for the kind of wedding reception every girl dreams of. Well, at least the kind of girl who dressed her dolls and even the family dog in matching outfits on rainy days and made them drink imaginary tea from tiny china cups.

Ruby had been such a girl, and these next few segments of her show would cover familiar territory. *Ruby's Relationship Rx* would focus on taming one woman's inner Bridezilla.

The problem was, Ruby wasn't certain she could handle the challenge.

She wasn't at all certain she could keep history from repeating itself. Today's couple had been arguing over the arrangements for their splashy wedding, much as Ruby had once done when she was engaged.

But this time there would be a happy ending. Ruby would show the bride the error of her spendthrift ways, while helping the groom to overcome his fear of commitment. Together, the couple would begin to enjoy the process of planning the wedding of their dreams, thanks to *Ruby's Relationship Rx.*

That was the theory, anyway.

The first segment would be taped in the oh-so-proper Stuyvesant Club, whose limestone façade and fusty interiors screamed Old Money and Fabulous Wedding.

Ruby should know. She'd booked the place once herself.

Armed with her new understanding of the Guy Point of View, however, Ruby hoped these hallowed halls wouldn't psyche her out. She might not have managed to pull off her own nuptials, but she would help her next guests do just that, thereby establishing her show as a solid hit. And once that happened, nobody would ever again refer to Ruby Lattingly as the Jilted Bride.

Because Ruby had learned from her mistakes and now understood that there was more to planning a wedding than a giant diamond, a fancy hall, and a designer dress.

Right?

She slipped out of the ballroom to the manager's office to await the arrival of today's guests, Ashley and Sten, already dubbed Bridezilla & Company for the bride's type A approach to wedding planning. If Ruby succeeded, Ashley and Sten would walk up the aisle one day soon to the strains of a quartet on loan from the Big Apple Orchestra, followed by a simply fabulous party worthy of a cover feature in *White Weddings* magazine.

All the elements for a happily-ever-after ending.

Except that the groom had cold feet.

And the bride was too consumed with planning her reception to notice.

Ruby's remedy called for them to dine by candlelight on a meal prepared to perfection by Chef Pierre Doumouchelles. Next up, his 'n' her shiatsu massages followed by a midnight carriage ride through Central Park.

It would be a night designed to remind the groom from

start to finish why he had proposed marriage in the first place. Straight out of Hutch's Guy Handbook.

Voilà. Problem solved, courtesy of *Ruby's Relationship Rx.*

Ruby's task was made easier by the fact that Ashley would not require a makeover. She was stunning, taller than tall with long blond hair. And she was thin. Not just regular thin. Long, sinewy arms and legs defined by muscle sculpted under the careful tutelage of a professional trainer.

Ashley Brooks was model thin.

Like Ruby once was.

Ruby reached instinctively for the belt at her waist and cinched it tighter. She wore a Diane von Furstenberg wrap dress that clung to her new curves, the ones that had developed over the last few months as the ice cream took its toll. It was an up-to-the-minute, retro seventies number with a bold geometric print, a hem that flared just above the knee, and a bow that tied delicately at the waist. Best of all, it had a V-neck that plunged all the way down to Ruby's new cleavage.

If Ruby was going to spend the day being filmed next to a girl who looked as if she was channeling Kate Moss, she might as well make the most of what she had. She yanked the neckline down as low as it would go.

"Wow."

She turned toward the sound of the familiar voice.

Hutch's big frame filled the space. He let out a low whistle and grinned, leaning against the doorway.

As though he wasn't going anywhere anytime soon. Ruby made a mental note to go back and buy a wrap dress in every color.

Hutch couldn't take his eyes off her. "That is one amazing dress."

Who needed the *South Beach Diet*? Ruby felt her cheeks turn warm. "Thanks," she murmured, looking down. She was not entirely comfortable with her new shape, but the look on Hutch's face told her she might be on to something. There might be advantages to having a Real Woman shape. Ruby smiled.

Hutch was smiling right back. "Wow," he said again. "Thanks again for Friday." He folded his powerful arms across his chest and crossed one foot in front of the other and rested it there, enjoying the view.

It was a power pose, and two weeks ago it would have annoyed Ruby. But today she just stood there, watching Hutch watch her. A warm feeling started down in her toes and welled up inside her till she felt the way she did after a long, luxurious bath. Without quite realizing she did so, Ruby stretched up on tiptoe so the gauzy fabric moved with her, and her golden hair cascaded around her neck. She giggled like a schoolgirl. "I had a good time."

Hutch closed the distance between them in one long stride. He was beside her in an instant, grabbing her hand, pulling her close enough to let her see the light shift inside those big hazel eyes that had suddenly turned serious. "How about you wear that dress tonight, and let me take you dancing?"

Ruby had always believed swooning was the stuff of

Victorian novels. Until now. The odd feeling in her knees made her realize it could be a thoroughly modern malady.

Luckily, Hutch had already positioned his free hand on the small of her back, ready to catch her if she fell.

So much for Ruby's Man Diet. Enough was enough. She was ready to move on. "Ah'll have to check my book to see if Ah'm free," she said, trying to lighten the mood with a mock southern drawl. "Ah'll have to check my dance card and get back to yew."

He smiled.

At this distance the manly scent of him filled Ruby's nostrils. She breathed in deeply.

Hutch lowered his face until it was inches from hers.

It was enough to make a talk show host forget she needed to keep her lipstick fresh for the camera.

"You check your book. Just remember to save the last dance for me." Hutch's voice dropped a notch, so there was no mistaking that his words were meant for her ears only.

Ruby would save him the last dance, and the first dance, and every one in between. She was about to tell him so, when Colin popped his head in the door.

Colin was pure evil at times, really.

"Our Bridezilla couple is finished with makeup. Shall I bring them to the ballroom?"

Ruby removed herself from Hutch and took a wobbly step back to clear her mind. "Yes. Show them to the ballroom. We'll meet you there."

Colin gave a quick nod but didn't leave. "You ready for this?"

"Of course."

"Seriously?" Colin raised an eyebrow, watching her.

Ruby scowled. Colin didn't believe she could pull this off. "Seriously," she said, banishing the warm-bath feeling in favor of pluck.

"Okay, then." He gave her the thumbs-up and left.

Ruby turned back to Hutch, aware that he had taken it all in. "Let's get to work. We have a hit show to tape."

Hutch grinned. "You bet we do, Ruby girl. I'm ready to roll." He wore a designer bowling shirt stylishly untucked over a pair of freshly pressed chinos.

Totally hip, in a Manly Man way.

"You can do this," he added quietly. "I know you can."

Ruby held his gaze for a moment, measuring him. She was used to flattery from men who wanted her for her beauty. But this was different. For one thing, Hutch was so handsome, he didn't need to play up to women to get what he wanted. No, he was looking at her as an equal, as a friend. And that was an entirely new experience for her. "Thanks," she said, aware that for the first time she really did feel she could do this.

She reviewed their guests' résumés for Hutch on the short walk to the ballroom. "He's a Wall Street guy, a hedge fund manager. She's from down South—your neck of the woods, I think."

"Texas?"

Ruby nodded.

Hutch grinned. "Then I guess that makes us old friends, 'cause you just know everyone in Texas knows everybody else." He winked.

Ruby smiled. "Okay, okay, I get it. Texas is a big place."

Even though they were off to a good start, Ruby's stomach gave a warning rumble as they approached the carved oak doors leading to the ballroom. She chalked it up to bad memories.

After today, she would be able to write the book on bad memories.

Ruby hesitated at the ballroom entrance. The oak-paneled walls, the flickering gas inset in the fireplace, the French doors hung with silk drapes, and the leaded crystal chandeliers were enough to touch off a bout of BPTSD (Bridal Post Traumatic Stress Disorder).

"You okay?" Hutch gave her elbow a squeeze.

"I'm fine," she lied.

He gave a quick smile and winked. "Hang tough."

She tried to smile back. "Right."

He surveyed the cavernous room. "This place gives me the creeps too."

Too. As though it was obvious that she was freaking out. In way over her head. She swallowed. "I don't have the creeps. No creeps. Why does everyone think this place gives me the creeps?"

Hutch cocked an eyebrow but didn't answer.

Ruby frowned. She had to admit that his hand was a steadying presence at her elbow. In terms of height alone, foot for foot Charles Begley Hutchinson IV was one big package of pure comfort. What he did next was so sweet and so tender that the feeling was supersized.

He reached out and smoothed a few strands of Ruby's hair back behind her ear. "You'll do fine," he said in a voice so low only she could hear. "You're doing okay

right now. Just remember, he's got a point of view too."
He smiled. "You can do this, Ruby. I'm on your side."

She believed him. "Thanks." She squared her shoulders,
lifted her chin, and waited.

"Here we are." Colin sailed in with Bridezilla & Company, freshly made up, miked, and ready to go. "Listen
up, everybody, I've got our new guests. This is Ashley
Brooks, our bride-to-be."

Ashley towered over Colin like an exotic marshland
bird, clad in a black Armani sheath dress that seemed to go
on for miles, with a long slit up the back to show her reed-
like legs.

The sort of dress that, until a month or two ago, Ruby
would have looked good in.

Ashley gave a dainty smile, dipping her pointy chin
down over her swanlike neck so her blond bangs slid down
over one eye.

À la Paris Hilton.

Ruby felt fat.

"And," Colin continued, "this is Ashley's fiancé, Sten
Wellingsworth, of Bedford, New York."

Sten flashed a smile, revealing the sort of too-precise
overbite that spoke of meticulous orthodontia. He wore a
gray flannel suit and a dull crimson tie with thick diagonal
stripes that were, no doubt, the dress colors from some
New Hampshire prep school where Mayflower descen-
dents could play lacrosse with their own kind.

Ashley draped one skinny arm around Sten, setting off
a proprietary jangle from her extensive collection of David
Yurman bracelets.

Ruby blinked in awe.

Ashley Brooks was more Ruby than Ruby. She had bagged the Big Game. She was about to climb onto the top rung of the career ladder of every aspiring model Ruby had ever met: She was Marrying Up.

Bridezilla & Company stood smiling like a pair of perfectly matched Herend figurines while Colin kept up a steady stream of small talk that was designed to put new guests at ease before taping began. "You've already met the host of the show, Ruby Lattingly. Ruby is short for Rachel Lucinda, but we all call her Ruby."

Flashing her professional talk-show-host smile, Ruby held her clipboard close to her midsection, hoping to appear thinner and in charge at the same time.

"And last but not least," Colin said, "is our star cameraman, on sabbatical from the news division, Charles Begley Hutchinson IV."

Ashley Brooks uttered a most unswanlike gasp.

The room turned silent.

Hutch just stared.

Ashley gripped her fiancé's arm so tightly, her silk tips were in danger of popping off.

"But you don't have to call him that," Colin continued smoothly. "You can call him—"

"Hutch." Ashley's voice was barely a whisper. Every bit of color drained from her face. She looked as if she had seen a ghost.

Maybe the ballroom *was* haunted.

"Hello, Ashley," Hutch said in a low, scratchy voice.

Leaving no doubt that this was not the first time they'd

met. In fact, from the looks of things, this was a cold case. Of the crimes-of-the-heart variety. As Ruby watched in stunned silence, Hutch morphed into the walking, breathing, worse-than-you-remember-from-the-photos member of the male species: Ashley's ex.

Hutch confirmed this by acting guilty. He swallowed, a move that required every muscle in his upper body, his Adam's apple bobbing slowly down till it hit bottom with an audible *thunk* before rising back up like the Times Square ball on New Year's Eve in reverse. As if the past had come back to haunt him.

The Cowboy Cameraman was stricken.

Eyes narrowing, Ruby remembered his bed with the hand-stitched quilt that had the interlocking wedding bands pattern. There was suddenly no question for whom it had been stitched.

Ashley Brooks glared at the room in general.

"Ashley," Hutch said again in a croak. He stepped forward, hand outstretched.

Ashley ignored the hand. "Allow me to introduce my fiancé, Sten Wellingsworth, president and CEO of Wellingsworth Partners," she said in a voice that could make Bethesda Fountain freeze on a summer day.

As if they hadn't all received an e-mail informing them of that fact.

Sten Wellingsworth grabbed Hutch's hand and pumped away. "Glad you're onboard, Hatch."

Hutch didn't bother to correct him. He was too busy doing that thing with his tongue inside his cheek.

"Actually, it's Hutch," Ruby said.

"All-righty then." Sten gave Hutch's hand one final, hearty shake.

The silence that followed could only be described as awkward.

Hutch and Ashley continued to stare and glare, respectively.

"Well," Ruby said, motioning in the air with her clipboard. "Let's get started. We have a lot of ground to cover."

Nobody moved.

"Let's get started," she repeated, using her in-charge tone. "We have a lot of relationship issues to discuss."

"I'll say," Hutch muttered.

Ashley Brooks' eyes narrowed. "Still as sarcastic as ever, I see."

Hutch's big shoulders sagged just a bit. "Sorry. I don't mean to be."

"You just can't help yourself," Ashley said in a cool voice.

"Anyhoo," Ruby began.

But nobody was listening.

Sten Wellingsworth cocked an eyebrow, looking from his bride-to-be to Hutch and back again. "You two *know* each other?"

Ashley's thin lips were sealed.

In observance of the primary rule of brides-to-be: The less said about one's past love life, the better. Especially when said past love life involved Charles Begley Hutchinson IV, aka the Cowboy Cameraman.

"Well," Ruby said, waving her clipboard like a white flag, "I think we should all just take our places and get started."

"Right," Colin echoed.

But Sten Wellingsworth refused to give up. "Where in the world did you two meet?"

It was, Ruby thought, the dumbest question he could possibly ask right now. Thereby proving that a diploma from a fancy New England prep school didn't boost a person's IQ. "Let's talk about old times later, shall we?"

"Don't tell me it was Iraq?" Sten tried to make it sound like a joke. But he wasn't smiling. When nobody answered, he tried again. "Well?"

"I've never been to Iraq," Ashley said finally. "We met way before that. Way before."

Emphasizing the word *way*. As though they'd met during the Paleozoic Era, before the likes of Hutch had learned to crawl onto dry land.

"A very long time ago," Hutch added helpfully.

"In Texas," Ashley said.

"I see." But Sten Wellingsworth did not look as though he saw anything. Not really.

"That's all in the past," Hutch said quietly.

"Yes," Ashley said.

The silence got louder and worked like a vortex, draining all the energy from the room until the place practically imploded around them. It was enough to make Ruby yearn for the days of vases hurtling across the set and birds dive-bombing. She cleared her throat noisily. "Okay, now that we've done the introductions, let's get started."

Nobody budged.

She tried again, careful to strike a positive tone. "We'll get the camera rolling and pan the room while we review your issues about your wedding day. We'll focus on those areas that we'd like to improve. Okay?"

Sten gave a tight nod, showing that half of Bridezilla & Company was onboard.

That was something.

Except for the fact that the other half was not.

Ashley's tiny lips were pursed in a not-so-tiny pout, her nose pointed high in the air in the direction of the leaded crystal chandeliers. "So, you want us to start by listing the things in the relationship that went wrong."

Wrong. The word hung in the air like letters on a string for a party decoration. A party from *H-E*-double hockey sticks.

Ashley continued to glare at Hutch.

"That's one way of looking at it," Ruby said in her most encouraging, it's-all-good tone of voice. "But I suggest another method. Let's start by coming up with ways to make this one wedding that everyone will talk about for years to come."

Hutch winced.

Thereby confirming Ruby's suspicion that Hutch had already been responsible for at least one wedding day that had gone down in the history of west Texas.

Which made Ruby want to do a little glaring at Hutch too.

Except that she had a hit show to tape. And this trip down memory lane was leading nowhere fast. "We've got one teeny, tiny little production issue to work out," Ruby said, grabbing Hutch. "So, if you'll excuse us, Colin will show you around."

"We'll start with a wine tasting," Colin said helpfully.

Ruby whisked Hutch to the empty manager's office and closed the door behind them.

He walked to the window and stood there, jangling the change in his pockets, staring down at the traffic on Fifth Avenue.

He was handsome, even from behind. It was a dumb thing to notice at a time like this, but there it was. Ruby realized even before she asked the question that she was hoping for a simple explanation. "Do you want to tell me about it?"

"Heck, no."

She sighed, her hopes dashed. And tried again. "Look, if there's something on your mind, let's talk about it and clear the air."

Wordlessly, he shook his head. The room was silent except for the jangling of change in his pockets.

The Cowboy Cameraman was reverting to type. Ruby had spent enough time with him to know that alpha males wanted to talk about their feelings as much as they wanted to cruise the sale rack for shoes on the second floor of Lord & Taylor. Which is to say, not much.

Ruby walked over and laid a hand on Hutch's shoulder. The muscles were rock hard underneath, as though Hutch could use a his 'n' hers shiatsu massage. "Come on, let's talk," she said softly. "You can tell me. I'll understand."

His only response was to continue staring down at Fifth

Avenue, where the jam-packed local bus had stopped to pick up more passengers before lumbering on its way.

"Look," Ruby said, trying to nudge him along, "I realize you and Ashley were an item once upon a time."

Hutch's silence told her this was one story that did not come with a fairy-tale ending.

"And maybe things didn't go the way you or she planned," Ruby continued. "But that's all in the past. We don't all marry our high school sweethearts, do we?" She recalled roly-poly Roland Weiser, the neighbor boy who had asked her to the junior prom only because their parents had put him up to it. The night had been awful. After graduation Roland slimmed down and got a nose job, dermabrasion for his acne scars, and a master's in international finance from Wharton. Today he ran the nation's largest health care holding company, owned a private island in the West Indies, and there was talk of a seat in the Senate. Ruby tried not to wince. "There's no point in regretting the past."

Except everybody did.

"Right," Hutch said at last.

But his shoulders were still as rock hard as the stone gargoyles above the club's entrance. And those gargoyles hadn't budged for nearly two centuries.

The bond Ruby had felt with Hutch when they shared that sweet, soulful kiss last night in the cab seemed broken now. "Look, we've got a show to tape," she said at last, trying not to think of the dozen staff members standing idle at that moment in the ballroom. Not to mention the sweating Alaskan king crab legs with mousseline.

"Everybody's depending on us to do our jobs. And I am your boss."

Bingo.

That roused him. Hutch stopped jangling and turned around. "How could I forget?" He smiled.

That was something. But it was a sad smile.

"I won't let you down, Ruby. I'm ready to work. Just remember, I never meant to disappoint you."

It sounded like good-bye. Ruby frowned. "You haven't done anything to disappoint me."

He shrugged. "Look, I'm here for you for as long as you'll have me."

But the look on his face told her he didn't think that would amount to much time at all.

"Well, then," Ruby said brightly. As though that settled it. But they both knew it did not.

"What went on between Ashley and me, is, uh, complicated," he said at last. "We dated for a while, but in the end, things didn't work out." He was careful to avoid meeting Ruby's gaze.

Ruby had a million questions to ask. She began with number one on her Top Ten List of Bad Things That Men Do. "Who ended it?"

Hutch shook his head. "It was a long time ago. I don't want to get into specifics."

Man Speak for: *I've been a very bad boy.* Eyes narrowing, Ruby proceeded to question number two. "How did it end?"

Hutch shrugged, raising his hands in the universal gesture for *Halt.*

As though he was practiced in the martial art of fending off direct attacks from angry women.

Not good. Ruby's eyes narrowed some more until they were like tiny chips of bluish glacial matter, and she didn't need a mirror to tell her she was back in Midtown Diva mode.

Shrugging, he drew in a deep breath and let it out. "Look, things between Ashley and me didn't turn out the way either of us would have liked. I did the best I could." His jaw was tight. "The best thing for right now is to do as you suggest. Leave the past in the past, and move on."

Indeed, that had been Ruby's suggestion. But tell that to the lump in her throat, which was back, along with the rumbling in her stomach. She didn't care to admit how disappointed she was that Hutch had no simple, easy explanation for what had gone on between him and Ashley Brooks, or how much she had wished he would turn out to be different.

But he wasn't. He was, after all, one of Them. A Man.

Ruby knew she wouldn't get any more answers from Hutch now. That was obvious. "Okay," she said, squeezing the words out past the lump. "Let's get to work."

Ruby Lattingly was, at her core, a practical woman.

The situation in the ballroom had gone downhill while they were gone.

Chef Pierre Doumouchelles was bullying his sous-chefs in rapid-fire French as they tried to blot the mousse-line sauce with napkins.

The wait staff stood around in nervous groups, whispering among themselves.

Worst of all was the sight of Ashley and Sten, sniffing corks, surrounded by empty wine bottles.

Ashley looked to be on edge.

Colin appeared fretful.

Sten seemed drunk.

Hutch took up his position behind the camera, a safe distance away.

Thank goodness for the zoom feature, Ruby thought, signaling Hutch to begin taping. "Greetings, all," she said as the red light flashed on. "And welcome back for a very special edition of *Ruby's Relationship Rx.*"

"You can say that again." Sten Wellingsworth hoisted his crystal goblet into the air.

Ruby ignored him. "Where we identify the problem, then prescribe a solution. Today, we brought our camera inside midtown's world-famous Stuyvesant Club for a sneak peek at the planning that goes into a superglam wedding reception."

Ruby thought she detected a low groan from behind the camera. But it might have been a taxi blowing its horn. She kept going. "Let's start with the happy couple, Ashley and Sten. Sten says that Ashley can't talk about anything but the wedding, and it's driving him crazy."

"You got that right." Sten waved his goblet through the air again.

"Shh," Ashley hissed.

Ruby continued. "And our bride-to-be says she only wants what every girl wants: the wedding of her dreams."

"It's becoming a nightmare," Sten growled.

Ashley hit him. Not hard, but she got him with an elbow to his side.

They could edit that out later, Ruby reasoned. "Ashley says Sten is no help. He's too busy trying to make the most of his remaining bachelor days."

Ashley tsk-tsked.

Ruby barreled through the rest of the intro she had rehearsed. "Can we put an end to this couple's Bridezilla blues? Let's meet them and see."

Motioning for a close-up, Ruby walked over to the wine tasting station.

Sten had unbuttoned the top of his shirt. His prep school tie was hanging loose and out of kilter. He smiled at Ruby and hiccupped.

Ruby ignored the sinking feeling in her gut. But there was no doubt about the fact that Sten Wellingsworth was definitely not ready for prime time.

"Let's begin with our bride-to-be, Ashley," Ruby said, determined to make this work. "I see you've been sampling the Rieslings to find one that will go with your seafood appetizer."

Ashley gave a sulky nod. "This wine is too sweet."

"Oh, and we can't have anything sweet around here," Sten said in a loud voice. "That would clash with the bride." He laughed at his own joke.

Nobody else did.

"I think we should go with something else, maybe a Chablis," Ashley said without skipping a beat, "because I think these grapes need drying out."

Drying out.

Sten didn't notice the insult that had been aimed straight at him. He was too busy trying to read the wine label.

Ruby heard a heavy sigh.

It was Hutch.

Ashley heard it too. "Oops, I forgot. The groom can do whatever he wants, but the bride is supposed to be perfect," she said, glaring at Hutch.

"And there you have it." Ruby kept her voice even, her eyes level with the camera. "Planning a wedding can be stressful." She paused for emphasis. "So, so very stressful. I mean, you can't imagine. But every woman who's ever done it knows what it's like to get caught up in the whole crazy process."

She tried to keep her tone light but failed. Painful memories were tumbling back, making it hard to stay focused. Ruby forgot where she was. Her words came faster and faster, her voice pitched higher and higher. "First, you reserve the church. Then you need to book the hall for the reception. You think you've got it all set. Then you find out the reception hall has been double-booked because of a problem they had with their software program. Their mistake. Your problem. So you go back to the church to see if they have another time open for the wedding service, and they don't. So you go back to the reception hall, around and around, because you've always known what you wanted. Then there's all this other stuff you need to decide. Like, do you have a sit-down dinner or buffet? And how many bridesmaids?"

Warming to her subject, Ruby began to wave her hands

in the air, unaware of the warning look Colin was sending her way.

Hutch was staring straight ahead.

Sten just watched, bewildered, his wine goblet temporarily forgotten.

Ashley was nodding in agreement, her chin going up and down like a bobblehead doll's.

Ruby took a deep breath and raved on. "And what about the bridesmaid dresses? What color? Who can help you decide? Not your mother, because she wants everything her way. Not your sister. Oh, no, not your sister. Because your sister doesn't speak to you. Why? Because she's two years older than you, she's been dating the same guy since college, and he still won't give her a ring. And now she's mad at you because you got engaged first! Like, whose fault is that?"

Ruby paused for a breath.

Colin was trying to get her attention, waving frantically as if he was hailing a cab in the rain. He made a slashing motion across his throat.

Ruby sniffed.

Colin mouthed the word, *Stop.*

But Ruby was caught in the grip of her memories. She had never given voice to her hurt, and so of course it had never had a chance to go away. She looked around the room now, seeking reassurance from the one man who had given her hope that the entire male species was not all bad.

Hutch would not meet her gaze. He was staring straight ahead.

The lump in Ruby's throat grew.

Sten picked up his wine goblet and motioned for a refill.

Ashley set her glass down hard. "I know exactly what you mean. Planning a wedding is a full-time job. Nobody appreciates how much there is to do. Nobody. Not even your own fiancé. When you need him the most, he pulls away. It is so very painful." She glared at Hutch.

Ruby knew just how Ashley felt.

Colin was waving a copy of the script in the air, the one they'd rehearsed together. But all Ruby could think of right now was the way Hutch was fussing with his camera, avoiding them both. Ruby and Ashley.

Ashley began to sniffle.

That did it.

"And the more you try to explain, the more your fiancé pulls away." The words bubbled up from a place deep inside Ruby where, she knew, they had been brewing for a long time. The words had been left unspoken since the day Ruby's own ex-fiancé broke off their engagement. He didn't stick around long enough to see the pain he had caused. "And in the end, all you have left is this, this"— Ruby gestured at the big ballroom—"monster of arrangements for a wedding that was never meant to be."

"And then it's too late," Ashley chimed in, her voice rising to a shriek. She had been kneading a section of the white linen tablecloth in her hands, turning it this way and that. Dropping it now, she jumped to her feet. "Because in your fiancé's mind, he's already gone. Checked out. But you don't know that. Oh, no, you don't have a clue about that. And do you know why?"

"Because he's not telling you the truth," Ruby said in

a voice rising with anger. "He's not telling you anything at all."

"Right!" Ashley was making her way over to the chef's table. She stopped to jab one long delicate finger into the air for emphasis. "That's right. No note. No e-mail. No calling you on the phone to say, 'We need to talk.' And do you know why?" She turned to Ruby, as though she was the talk show host and Ruby was the guest in need of advice.

"Because," Ruby replied, her voice barely above a whisper, "guys hate to talk." She moved across the ballroom after Ashley, as though Ashley was the Pied Piper of Hamelin.

The ballroom was now deadly quiet.

"Right again!" Ashley kept walking.

Ruby followed. They reached the table with the platter of Alaskan king crab legs in mousseline sauce.

The sous-chefs stopped blotting and scattered. Even Chef Pierre Doumouchelles backed off.

"And so your first clue is your last." Ashley spat the words out, staring at Hutch.

"Right," Ruby nodded. The lump in her throat was so big, it was hard to squeeze the words past, but they tumbled out anyway. "One day, you're planning your wedding. And the next, you wake up and he tells you it's over and that's it. He's met someone else. And he realizes he never really knew what love was until he met her, this Other Woman. And so he's going to leave you. It's a personal growth step—for him!" A sob rose up in Ruby's throat, turning that lump into a big, hot hockey puck.

"No!" Ashley shrieked.

"Huh?" Ruby sniffed uncertainly.

"That is not what happens," Ashley exclaimed, jabbing that finger into the air again for emphasis so that her David Yurman bracelets jangled and jumped.

"No?" Ruby glanced from Ashley to Hutch, who looked as if he wished he were someplace else. Anywhere but here.

"It plays out much, much worse than that." Ashley's voice had dropped ominously low. "He doesn't drop you for someone else."

Horror reduced Ruby's voice to a whisper. "What does he do?" But she already knew. There was a chill in the air, the kind you felt when you stayed too long in the produce aisle at D'Agostino's on a hot day.

Ashley stretched her arm out as far as it could go.

Her bony finger was aimed straight at Hutch. "Ask Hutch! He'll tell you the worst way to leave a woman."

Hutch was staring down at the carpet, as though the answer to that question was written there in the plush fleur-de-lis pattern.

The temperature in the room dropped even lower, to somewhere around absolute zero.

"Tell us," Ruby echoed, her voice sounding tinny and far away to her own ears.

At last, Hutch looked up at Ashley and shook his head sadly. "I tried to tell you, Ashley, I really did, but you were so busy with . . . everything." He motioned helplessly at the room in general, taking it all in, from the Michelin-starred chef to the fresh-cut orchids to the highly polished silverware.

"You tried to tell me? Hah!" Again Ashley spat her words out. Her entire body shook with anger from the top of her golden highlighted hair down to the tips of her must-have, leopard-print mules. Reaching out to steady herself, Ashley closed her hand on the silver platter of Alaskan king crab legs. "You didn't try hard enough, Hutch."

"Ashley, please don't do this." Hutch left the camera running and stepped around in front of it, raising his hands to try to calm Ashley. His tone was pleading. "You didn't deserve what I did. And I'm sorry. Not a day goes by that I don't regret how I acted. But you have a new life and a new love. We don't need to talk about it now."

Ashley cut Hutch off. "You never told me you changed your mind about our wedding. You just decided not to show up. You left me at that altar all alone!"

Ashley's words summoned up the pain of Ruby's own broken engagement. Lights danced before Ruby's eyes, and the room started to sway. She reached out to steady herself on the table.

"Charles Begley Hutchinson the fourth," Ashley intoned, sounding out each syllable as though she were handing down a sentence in criminal court, "you are guilty of the worst possible breakup. You left me standing at the altar!"

In the end, it was Ruby who picked up the platter and flung it at Hutch's head.

He took it like a Manly Man.

The ballroom was silent except for the sound of the silver tray bouncing onto the floor, scattering Alaskan king crab legs everywhere.

Hutch stood stock-still, like an infantryman at inspection. After a time, he scooped a fingerful of mousseline sauce into his mouth and sucked thoughtfully, watching Ruby with mournful eyes. "Guess this means I take a rain check for tonight."

Chapter Fourteen

Leonard Klingston was hunched over his BlackBerry when Ruby stormed in and flounced into the chair across from his desk. "Have a seat," he said, without looking up. "You know much about these?"

Ruby scowled. Today had been another disaster. Ruby had fought her way through a knot of paparazzi waiting outside the cable network's entrance. They all wanted a shot of the Jilted Bride after her latest failure. Ashley and Sten had left the Stuyvesant Club without a word. The chef was furious about the loss of his king crab dish. Not to mention that Ruby had been handed a hefty bill for carpet cleaning.

None of which was the real reason Ruby felt like crying.

That had to do with Hutch. The only man Ruby had been tempted to trust again had turned out to be the biggest cad in the tristate area. He had wooed her into trusting him, with all his sexy, Manly Man talk about sincerity and fidelity. Hah! The man's picture should be hanging in every post office in America.

And Klingston was playing with his BlackBerry.

Typical man. "Only the basics," Ruby admitted through gritted teeth.

"Never mind." Shrugging, he started to fiddle with a stack of pink message slips on his desk.

On top was a call from Page Six at the *New York Post.* No doubt fishing for a quote about the latest dustup on the set of *Ruby's Relationship Rx.*

Good. The more paparazzi, the merrier, Ruby thought grimly. Klingston would be aggravated by them. And the more aggravated Klingston got, the more likely it was that he would grant Ruby her wish.

And her wish was simple. She wanted Hutch fired.

Ruby had thought things through after Bridezilla & Company stormed out of the Stuyvesant Club ballroom that morning, then thought about it some more when she followed suit. She'd had plenty of time to fume in the cab ride back to network headquarters.

And the facts were simple. Ruby had suspected that Hutch was hiding something in his past. But she'd never dreamed until that moment in the ballroom that he'd done something as cruel as jilting a bride at the altar.

The thought of it even now made Ruby twitch. She shifted in her seat, deciding it was time to break out the heavy artillery. Because when Ruby was finished with Klingston here today, Hutch would be out of a job and, more important, out of her life.

Leaning forward, she yanked at the V-neck on the von Furstenberg wrap dress so it revealed her cleavage. "I know we've had our ups and downs, and I came to make a suggestion as to how we can move forward to make things right."

"So, let me guess. Today's show got messy, Bridezilla and Company went packing, and now you want to ditch them and find a new couple to work with?" Klingston looked up for the first time, right past Ruby's décolleté.

This was bad.

"Basically," Ruby replied.

"No deal."

"I think it might be time for a new cameraman as well. Hutch is best suited for the hard news division." It would be a perfect match for his hard head.

"Nope." Klingston resumed fiddling with his Black-Berry.

Unbelievable.

"But . . ." Ruby began. Her show was practically on the skids, and he was fiddling with his BlackBerry.

It was downright Barbaric.

"Um, Leonard?" Ruby waited till he looked up, then raised one hand and flicked her hair so her bracelets jangled in her classic signature move. She'd been practicing this move since freshman year at college, when she had discovered its hypnotic effect on the male of the species.

But not on Klingston. He stared, unblinking, from his Aeron chair.

It occurred to Ruby that Leonard Klingston didn't care how beautiful she was, nor did he care about how difficult her morning had been. This, no doubt, was the iron quality that had earned him the name The Barbarian.

Not a comforting thought.

Ruby tried not to stammer. "I think it's best for all concerned if we move on—find a new couple to work with and a new cameraman."

"No deal. Keep Hutch. Work things out with Bridezilla and Company."

"That's not possible," Ruby protested. "I need to find another couple, for one thing."

"One you can save?"

"Basically," she said at last. "After what happened today, I'm not sure I can help Bridezilla and Company stay together."

"Doesn't matter. If they break up, if they stay together, we win either way." Klingston drummed his meaty fingers on his glass desk, leaving a smudge.

Ruby stared, uncomprehending. But Klingston's next words left no doubt as to his meaning.

"Your show is hot. The only weakness we saw in beta testing was when you got that Golf Couple to kiss and make up. Happy couples are boring." Klingston paused to let his meaning sink in.

"You made it onto the local news at midday with your temper tantrum at the Stuy Club, and my money says you'll be on again at five o'clock." Klingston fingered his stack of phone messages. "Based on the calls I'm getting, you'll make Page Six in tomorrow's *Post,* and probably the *Daily News*, *New York Magazine,* and maybe even *Entertainment Weekly.*"

Klingston let out a happy sigh. "I can see the headlines now: 'Jilted Bride Strikes Again.' Another breakup. I like it."

Ruby stared, numb with disbelief. "You're not saying you hope this couple breaks up on my show?"

One look at his face told it all.

Ruby's eyes widened in horror.

Klingston smiled, revealing thick rows of flattopped teeth that looked as if they were meant for grinding fresh leaves or raw grain.

The man was positively prehistoric.

He fixed her with his beady, deep-set eyes and leaned forward until she got a whiff of something resembling wet earth. "Honey, breaking up is what made you famous in the first place. Why do you think we signed you?"

The chilly feeling came back and settled in her bones. Ruby shivered so hard, her teeth chattered, making speech impossible. She shook her head, at a loss for words.

"There's more buzz about *Ruby's Relationship Rx* than I ever dreamed of," Klingston said happily. "The numbers are great. Your show just keeps getting better and better. It's why I sent Bridezilla and Company your way in the first place. I wanted to see what you'd do with a woman whose wedding was out of control."

He paused for effect. "You know the type."

Because you are the type. Ruby shook her head. "But it's not what you think. I know I can help Ashley and Sten decide what's best for them. I know I can get some good footage of them."

"Then do it." Klingston leaned forward. "Sten's bachelor party is coming up this weekend. Tape it."

It was the last thing Ruby wanted to do, not with Hutch manning the camera, anyway. She pressed on with her cause. "The problem is Hutch, our cameraman. There's a chemistry problem between Hutch and Ashley, not between Hutch and me."

Except there was.

Klingston smiled, stretching his lips to reveal his gums. He looked scarier than usual when he smiled.

Ruby shrank back in her seat.

"Get Hutch to film that bachelor party," Klingston snapped. "It makes for good TV. And if they break up, well, it's what we expected from you all along."

The room took a dizzying tilt. Ruby had once read that the Empire State Building swayed a little bit every time a sparrow flew into it. She couldn't remember why but decided that all skyscrapers must be designed that way, because Klingston's office seemed to be shaking right now. Or maybe it was Ruby's world that was turning upside down. "You don't mean you expected me to fail?" she stammered at last.

But Klingston had already gone back to his BlackBerry, signaling that the meeting had ended. "I say keep doing what you're doing. Film a segment on Bridezilla and Company's bachelor party. Let 'er rip. Then we'll see about assigning you a new cameraman."

He wasn't called The Barbarian for nothing.

Chapter Fifteen

Ruby held her hands out to admire them. "Not bad. How's yours?"

Ashley Brooks looked down at her fingers and gave a quick nod. "It's a good manicure. Ballet Slippers is not my usual color, but I like it."

"Very bridal," Ruby observed, taking a sip of her Diet Coke.

"Very bridal," Ashley agreed, taking a sip of her own Diet Coke.

Happy Hour was in full swing at the Beauty Bar, the lower Manhattan watering hole known for its retro beauty-parlor interior and full-service martini manicures. It was the perfect place for a rendezvous between an up-and-coming talk show host and an ambitious bride-to-be guest.

Ruby's game plan was to loosen up Ashley with some girly-girl bonding time here at the Beauty Bar before heading uptown for a surprise visit to Sten's bachelor party, which was being filmed at that very moment by Hutch.

They would combine the bachelor party footage with the outtakes shot yesterday in the Stuyvesant Club ballroom for a segment on how to put some spice back into a relationship that was straining against the stress of wedding plans run amok. They would film the bride enjoying some girl time, getting a manicure, and the groom enjoying some guy bonding time at his bachelor party. Apparently, key ingredients to a happy wedding.

And in the process Ruby would regain control of a talk show gone mad. That was the plan, anyway.

Ruby fished the last cashews from a bowl of cocktail nuts, careful not to smudge her newly varnished silk tips. She offered the bowl to Ashley, who shook her head.

"If I gain even one ounce, my wedding gown won't fit."

Ruby gave an understanding nod as though she, too, was watching her weight. But the fact was, the rumbling in her stomach had grown so loud since yesterday, she'd hardly done anything but eat. She'd left Klingston's office feeling completely drained, stopping at a street vendor for a hot pretzel slathered in mustard for the cab ride home. Dinner was takeout from her neighborhood Chinese, a combo complete with white rice, full-strength soy sauce, and even spicy wonton noodles, followed by half a package of Chips Ahoy. They were even better dipped in peanut butter. Who knew?

Ruby blamed the restless night that followed on the MSG in her take-out food. She'd had another strange dream about Texas, a state that had never figured on her

list of must-see vacation destinations. This time, she was
floating just above those fields scented with sage, pumping mightily at unseen wings to keep every inch of alti-
tude. She whirled along, breathing deeply, taking in great
lungfuls of sweet air, yearning to go higher and higher
still so she could float far above the canyon floor with its
pinyons and red oaks.

Pinyons? Red oaks?

Ruby wouldn't know a red oak from a blue, ecru, or
fuchsia oak. But this was a dream, after all, and anything
was possible. What felt real was the triumph she felt inside.

*"A man doesn't just get bored and leave, Ruby, not
when he knows what's in his heart."*

Hutch was there, or at least his voice was, filling her
ears and her mind, beckoning her back. She took one last,
deep breath, wishing she could hold that floating feeling
inside her forever.

She had landed with a bump and woke up moments before the alarm rang that morning. She'd lain in bed, gathering strength for the tough day ahead.

She didn't mind working with Bridezilla & Company.
She had always liked a challenge. She didn't even mind
the fact that Klingston had set her up. She liked to prove
people wrong.

No, what bothered Ruby was being forced to work with
Hutch. At the moment, she never wanted to lay eyes on
Charles Begley Hutchinson IV again.

She'd slid out of bed more determined than ever to prove
once and for all that she was no longer the jinxed Jilted
Bride, doomed to break up every happy couple she met.

Much later, when she remembered the events of this day, she would remember the dream of flight and how, even after she showered and hailed a taxi to take her downtown, her nostrils were full of the scent of sage.

"This place is fun," Ashley pronounced, looking around the room, which was jammed with Happy Hour clients sitting under retro fifties domed hair dryers. "Who knew it was here?"

Ruby nodded. East Fourteenth Street was well off the beaten track for women like her and Ashley. But she had learned there was a whole, big world beyond the Upper East Side. Like Sylvia's, for one thing, a place she'd heard of and never visited until Hutch . . . The thought of him tugged at Ruby's insides. She pushed the thought away. She was Hutch's boss. That was it. Pure and simple. End of story. She checked her watch. "We need to leave soon."

Ashley blew on her nails. "Good. These are almost dry."

"We've got a big night ahead. We'll get some great footage."

"Good." Ashley looked doubtful. "Tell me again why dropping in on Sten's bachelor party is such a good idea?"

Ruby couldn't admit the truth, which was that Klingston had insisted on it. "Because you need to put some pizzazz back into your relationship," she said instead. "Just kind of join in the fun so you can prove to your fiancé that you're not so caught up in planning your wedding that you've forgotten how to have a good time. And we'll get some great footage for our segment on your reception."

Ashley brightened. "It will be a nice keepsake."

Really, they were like sisters separated at birth.

Ashley tapped her pinkie nail gingerly. "Dry," she pronounced. "You're sure Sten won't mind a surprise visit?"

Ruby looked up from her own silk tips. "Not a chance. He's got nothing to hide. After all, he's allowing us to film it. Colin and Hutch are there right now."

Hutch. Just saying his name made them both flinch.

"It's too bad he's still assigned to us," Ashley began.

"We're stuck with him for now," Ruby said. "Thank you for bearing with me."

Ashley shrugged, toying with the pink wrapper from one of the packets of artificial sweetener she had used in her iced tea. "Actually, seeing him yesterday helped. It felt good to get it all out. I hadn't seen him since that day . . ." Her voice trailed off.

"It was a long time ago," Ruby said quickly.

"True. But I've had this feeling of déjà vu since yesterday in the Stuyvesant Club."

"Déjà vu? Like how?" But the prickly feeling on the back of Ruby's neck was already providing the answer.

Ashley sighed. "Seeing Hutch again yesterday brought it all back, and I couldn't help but remember things he said when we were engaged."

"Such as?"

"Such as, there were signs all along that we weren't meant for each other, but I ignored them. Instead, I got caught up in trying to plan the perfect wedding. It was easier than facing the fact that Hutch and I just weren't meant for each other." She sighed. "Don't get me wrong. He's a great guy. He's loyal and sweet and gifted. I love the way he takes pictures of the world around him so he can share it with other people."

"And he has a way of making you feel that you're okay just the way you are." The words slipped out before Ruby even noticed she was saying them.

Ashley gave her an understanding look. "You know, I was young and spoiled and just not ready to be married. If I had it to do over, I'd think long and hard before I'd give up on a man like Hutch."

Ruby looked around the Beauty Bar and wondered if those old hair dryers still worked properly, because the place suddenly felt far too warm. "You've got plans to marry another wonderful man," she said, changing the subject.

Ashley nodded. "But I'm faced with the same situation, which is why I wanted to come onto your show in the first place. I just got way too busy with these wedding plans. It's my old pattern, I guess. Maybe there's something I need to take a closer look at." She gave a small smile. "I guess it took yesterday in the Stuyvesant Club to remind me of what Hutch told me back then—that I was too preoccupied with our wedding. I was so busy trying to make everything perfect that he felt I would never be happy living with him, because he's not perfect and never will be." Ashley's fingers were busy folding the tiny pink wrapper into halves, then quarters, then eighths, and so on, until it formed a perfect, teeny square.

Ashley dropped the square and gave Ruby a look of despair. "The problem is, Sten's been saying the same thing."

Déjà vu must be contagious, because Ruby's onetime

fiancé had said all those things once too. He had planned a surprise getaway for them right before the wedding. Ruby had canceled at the last minute, in favor of her gown fitting.

"You know what the funny thing is?" Ashley leaned in close. "I waited all these years to tell Hutch how wrong he was, and now that I finally have the chance, I'm not so sure." She blinked back tears.

Ruby fanned Ashley quickly with a napkin and made soothing sounds. No point in ruining anyone's eye shadow this early in the night. But Ashley's next words made Ruby worry for them both.

Ashley took a gulp of her cola and tried to collect herself. "The truth is, Hutch was a great guy. He was sweet and kind and fun. All he ever wanted was to have someone to love who wouldn't fuss at him too much. Someone who would just let Hutch be Hutch, I suppose."

"Yeah," Ruby said faintly. If Ashley was ready to forgive the man who'd left her standing at the altar, where did that leave Ruby?

"I hope you can help me. I just don't want to make the same mistake again with Sten."

Ruby mustered a reassuring tone that she did not feel. "Tonight will change a lot of things. Just wait. You'll see."

Chapter Sixteen

Hutch watched Sten's bachelor party through the lens of his camera and scowled. It was amazing how rotten he could feel in the midst of such merriment.

"Hey, Hatch, try one!" Sten Wellingsworth came his way, toting a cache of French champagne with the corks still intact and Havanas fresh from the humidor.

"Thanks, pal, but I'm working." Hutch zoomed in for a close-up of Sten, who looked every inch the ex-frat boy who was the life of the party. He wore a buttoned-down striped Oxford (sans prep school tie), baggy Wranglers, and Hush Puppies.

Angling back, Hutch got a wide view of a roomful of guys who were dressed pretty much alike, boogying to "Rock Lobster," which blared from speakers buried in the walls—standard equipment in Fifth Avenue penthouses like this one.

Hutch stifled a yawn. He'd spent a sleepless night. As of yesterday, Ruby knew the truth. And Hutch was pretty sure she hated his guts right now. So much for a chance at real love with a woman who managed to be plucky, smart, and pretty enough to turn heads all at the same time. He needed to revert to SOP (standard operating procedure). Namely, stick to one-date wonders and bury himself in work.

Starting now. He panned the camera around Sten's penthouse apartment, thinking of Ashley Brooks. Unless she had changed her stripes, she would have a field day decorating this place once she was married. Out with the old, in with the new. Beginning with that black leather sofa littered with empty peanut shells and guys swilling their beverages straight from the can.

They took turns bouncing on a whoopee cushion, to peals of raucous laughter.

Hutch rolled his eyes. *Better you than me, Sten, ol' pal.* But Hutch knew in his heart he didn't mean it.

Now "Rock Lobster" blasted at full volume.

Sten hit the polished oak floor, literally, in a fairly decent Worm.

Someone dimmed the lights, to general hooting and hollering all around.

Hutch switched his camera to night vision.

Someone banged on the front door.

Sten was too busy squirming on the hardwood floor to notice.

But he froze when he saw who it was.

So did every other guy in the room.

Hutch was so surprised, he left the camera rolling in autofocus.

There in the doorway was Kristal, her sequins shimmying like a burlesque dancer's in Vegas.

Hutch's onetime on-again, off-again, good-times gal pal.

"Hey, guys, is this a private party, or can anyone join in the fun?" Kristal shook her leotard, giving those sequins an extra shimmy.

There was a general roar of approval.

Kristal stepped inside and got down to business.

Hutch felt his gut twist as if someone had thrown a punch dead center. It was not a good feeling. He shot Colin a questioning look.

Colin had been keeping well out of camera range in the shadows at the edge of the room, clutching his clipboard like a security blanket. He caught Hutch's look and shook his head vigorously from side to side, as if to say, *Don't blame me. I had nothing to do it with it.*

Hutch believed him. But If Colin hadn't hired Kristal to come here tonight, who had? Hutch's jaw tightened as he worked the lens for a wide-angle shot. And he didn't like what he saw.

Kristal had brought her own CD, cued to "Groove Is in the Heart." The partygoers were forming a circle around her and Sten, applauding, egging them on. Ol' Sten was having the dance of his life.

Hutch sighed. It wasn't that he minded watching Kristal do her thing. He knew how she earned a living. And, heck, she was pretty good at it. You had to hand it to a gal who brought her own cowbell to a party and wasn't afraid to use it.

Fact was, Hutch's feelings had never run deep for Kristal.

Nope, the problem Hutch had at the moment was the floor-licking grin on Sten Wellingsworth's face.

He was enjoying this too much.

Ashley didn't deserve a guy like this. Not after what she'd been through the first time she was engaged, thanks to Hutch.

Never mind how Ruby would react when she viewed the outtakes. She'd be madder than a wet hen.

And that, Hutch knew, would be bad. He should know. He had grown up on the second biggest cattle ranch in Texas. They'd kept a few hens in back of the kitchen garden, and those hens were no fun in the rainy season. No fun at all.

Hutch groaned, but it couldn't be heard above the music. "Locomotion" was now pounding through the high-def sound system. The song was a classic, that was something. Maybe this night wouldn't turn out so badly after all.

He saw in a moment how wrong he was.

The partygoers rearranged themselves into one long conga line with Kristal and Sten at the lead.

Heading for the master bedroom suite.

Colin gave Hutch a helpless look, still clutching his clipboard.

Hutch unlatched his camera from the tripod and followed.

Sten let out a war whoop and boogied on.

The line of dancing guests snaked through the bedroom and into a large bathroom, complete with a bubbling, steaming hot tub.

Hutch's gut wrenched tighter, twisted by an unseen hand.

Colin's face had a look of pure panic.

Hutch knew just how he felt.

This night was about to get worse, much worse.

Kristal popped off one of her shoes, and it sailed through the air and landed at Hutch's feet. You didn't see shoes like that except on *The Wizard of Oz*. The other one followed soon after.

Kristal hollered something, but it was difficult to hear over the stereo, which was now blaring "Yellow Submarine" at full volume. She shimmied herself down into the hot tub, to wild applause from the assembled guests. "Who's up for a little hot tub action?"

The answer was obvious.

Sten Wellingsworth had already slipped off his Hush Puppies and removed the wallet from his hip pocket. He jumped right in, clothes and all. "Do those sequins shake when they're wet?" he roared.

Hutch knew he needed to take action, fast.

He did something next that he had never done in all his life. Not even when he was a little boy, dangling mortally close to the edge of the bull pen's split-rail fence with his dad's ancient Polaroid Swinger wrapped around one wrist, trying for the best possible close-up.

Hutch laid his camera down. "Sten, you really don't want to do this."

"Why is that?" Sten said, cozying up to Kristal.

Hutch swallowed, searching for words. Ashley could be fussy, sometimes downright prissy. She hadn't been the right match for Hutch, and it was possible she wasn't the right match for Sten. Hutch didn't know. But he was certain of one thing. She didn't deserve this. "It's just not right," he said at last.

"Hutch, all the fun's gone right out of you since the last time we met. You could use a little soak in the hot tub yourself." Kristal giggled.

At least she didn't hold a grudge.

"Two's company, three's a crowd," Sten grumbled, waving everyone away. He turned to Kristal. "What say we make this into a private party?"

"Sten, you need to think of Ashley," Hutch began. He grabbed a towel and made a move toward the tub.

"Why? She'll never know the difference," Sten replied.

But a voice from the back of the crowd near the door proved him wrong.

"Don't count on it," Colin said, elbowing his way inside. He had the look of a man in the path of a herd of stampeding cattle. "She's here."

"What?" Sten tore himself away from those sequins.

"Yoo-hoo! Honey, we're here! Surprise!" Ashley's voice trilled from the hallway. "What are you doing in there?"

Sten's eyes rolled open, wide and white, as he looked around the room in panic. "Hide me," he hissed.

But it was too late.

There was a general murmuring from the crowd near

the bathroom door as the newest guests began to squeeze their way inside.

"Come out, come out, wherever you are," Ashley called.

"Help," Sten whispered.

"Do something," Colin urged.

Being the sort of man he was, Hutch did.

He threw himself into the hot tub with a mighty splash, landing precisely in between Kristal and Sten.

He came up for air in time to see Ruby and Ashley elbow their way to the front of the crowd and get their first glimpse of the hot tub.

If looks could kill, the party would end three guests short.

And Hutch would be the first to go.

Chapter Seventeen

Ruby stared.

The scene rendered her speechless. Hutch in a hot tub with Sten. And Kristal, a woman Ruby had met just once but remembered all too well.

It was impossible to forget a woman in a sequined, leopard-print leotard.

Just as, even now, it was impossible not to notice that Hutch could have passed for the cover shot of *People* magazine's Sexiest Man Alive issue. His wet hair clung to his face in a way that served to accentuate that granite jaw. His clothes were streaming wet, revealing the lines of broad shoulders and what looked to be washboard abs.

Ruby hated herself for noticing those things at a time like this.

Hutch's eyes were locked on hers, beseeching her with an unspoken plea.

179

Ruby looked away.

The room emptied out. Even Colin was gone. And Kristal was following fast, stopping just long enough to cover those sequins with a towel. Someone pulled the plug on the music.

The bathroom went silent, save for the rumbling of the hot tub jets.

Sten was the first to speak, making his case to Ashley. "Sweet pea, I know how this must look."

"Don't tell me any lies," Ashley sputtered, two bright spots of red appearing high on her cheeks.

"I'm not lying," Sten protested. "Hatch and Kristal were in the hot tub. I reached in to pull the plug, slipped, and fell in on top of them."

"Give me a break," Ashley snapped.

Hutch cleared his throat. "It's true. I was filming the party and got carried away when Kristal arrived. I wound up in here for old times' sake, I guess. Sten was trying to put things in order. He slipped and fell in. That's all." He didn't meet Ruby's gaze.

Ashley sniffed. "Really?"

"Really." Sten jumped from the hot tub, his socks squelching on the tiled floor, and pulled Ashley to him in a soggy embrace.

"Oh, darling, I'm so relieved," Ashley said, her voice muffled in Sten's shirt. "I don't know how I could have accused you of being such a, such a . . ."

"Womanizer," Ruby said in a flat voice. She glared at Hutch.

He climbed from the tub, one overflowing cowboy boot

at a time, and stood with water cascading off him like some giant garden sculpture. His eyes were round and big with pleading, his gaze locked on Ruby's. Water spilled from the tops of his cowboy boots onto the floor.

It wouldn't take much of a push to send him back into the tub.

But that wouldn't change anything.

Ruby contented herself with giving him her best Ice Princess glare.

He looked suitably sorry, his face covered in a hangdog look. "Can we talk? Alone?"

Ruby let her shoes provide the answer. She turned on her heel and left, not even slowing down in the living room, where Colin was gathering sound equipment and rolling up wires.

He tried to flag her down. "Boss, it's not what you think."

"Save it," Ruby barked. She wasn't in the mood. After all, Colin was one of Them. A Man.

She pushed the elevator button so hard, one of her silk tips snapped, giving her yet another reason to end this night as quickly as possible.

As though she needed one.

The doors slid open, and she stepped inside, hearing a squishing sound close behind.

Ruby sighed.

Hutch squelched aboard as she jammed the button marked *L.*

Ruby stared at the display panel as the car began its descent.

Hutch cleared his throat. "Look, I know what you must be thinking."

"Somehow, I doubt that." Ruby regretted the words as soon as she uttered them. Speaking to Hutch would only encourage him. She stared straight ahead at the display showing the numbered floors.

Hutch sighed. "I know the way I treated Ashley was inexcusable, ending our engagement the way I did."

Against her will, Ruby harrumphed.

"But I was much younger then," he continued. "I felt I had no choice. No matter how many times I tried to get her attention, I failed. In the end, I knew I could never make her happy."

The temptation was too much. Ruby whirled to face Hutch, keeping her chin high in the air. "So you left her standing at the altar? Is that Man Speak for 'I fell out of love with you'?"

"No. I didn't fall out of love. I just realized I had never been in love in the first place." Hutch stared down at the puddle that had formed at his feet. "Maybe it just took all that frou-frou wedding stuff for me to realize it. Maybe things worked out for the best in the end, after all." Hutch lifted his gaze and looked at Ruby.

The question in those hazel eyes had a warming effect on that ice shelf deep inside Ruby, and it shifted, resulting in one of those giant fissures you saw on *National Geographic* specials about global warming. She felt herself start to yield.

Hutch must have sensed it, because he ventured one step closer. "I made amends, in my own way. I kept my distance from every woman I met so I would never hurt anyone in the same way again. It worked pretty well for a while."

Until the day he met Ruby. Ruby sensed that was what he was getting at. Sensed it and pretended not to. "Until you lost control and jumped into a hot tub with your old girlfriend," she said coolly.

"No," he protested.

"But you can't help it. You're a man."

Shaking his head, Hutch gave up on words and pulled Ruby into his arms.

Despite her tough talk, Ruby didn't put up a fight. She wanted to, out of sheer habit. But that was the only reason, she realized, just old habit.

"No, you've got it all wrong," he said, holding her steady so she had no choice but to look deep into his eyes. "I thought this would be a cushy assignment. I never figured that working on *Ruby's Relationship Rx* would challenge everything I thought about women." His voice dropped a notch or two. "Maybe we could learn something from each other."

Hutch's words were straight out of Ruby's fantasy, the one in which she would meet a man who was sensitive and not afraid to show it, brave when it came to admitting he still had a lot to learn. Not intimidated by her. A cowboy of the heart.

The air between them was crackling with some sort of energy.

Ruby gave up. What she wanted in that moment more than anything was to close the tiny space that remained between them, and so she did. She relaxed against him, feeling him, warm and still damp from the hot tub. She didn't care.

She lifted her face to his and allowed herself to be wrapped tightly in his arms in a kiss that went on and on. His breath was warm on her face, his lips strong and gentle and sweet all at the same time, pulling her closer. Ruby wanted in her heart for that kiss to last forever, even though her mind told her it was not a good idea.

The elevator landed with a gentle thump, and the doors slid open.

"Evening, folks," the doorman said with barely a glance. "Need a cab?"

As though it was the most natural thing in the world to see a couple headed out on an autumn night in New York, one dry and one dripping wet.

Hutch pulled his lips off Ruby's. "Yeah, we'll share it."

Despite what Ruby was about to do, the memory of Hutch's lips on hers lingered, playing in her dreams all through the restless night that followed, like rays of light bouncing off shadows of doubt that would not go away.

"Please make that two," she said stiffly, pushing Hutch away. "We need separate cabs."

Chapter Eighteen

She had the dream again but didn't remember it until she was in Klingston's office the next morning.

"We need to make some changes at *Ruby's Relationship Rx*. Starting with Hutch. We need to reassign him. It would calm things down on the set," Ruby said.

And in my heart.

Klingston shrugged. "Done."

Ruby had braced herself for a fight. "Done?"

"He's already gone. Staff doc gave him the all-clear, so he's good to go. He came in here early this morning looking to get off your show. He's probably headed to JFK right about now."

So Hutch had beat her to it. He was gone. It was what Ruby thought she wanted. So why did she feel as if she had been jilted all over again? She gulped. "I see." Except she didn't.

"I got you a new cameraman, and you can have anything else you need." Klingston tapped the remote to his giant plasma-screen TV. "Because the outtakes from yesterday are dynamite. I mean they're really, really good. One more breakup. The test audience will go wild."

This was the man who had set her up to fail.

And that's when it hit Ruby. She remembered the dream. She'd had it again last night. In it, she was floating, through a sky that was impossibly blue, above a hot prairie that stretched away as far as she could see. She was flying.

The air around Klingston's desk vibrated with the force of ten thousand wings. She waited to see if he felt it.

"You need anything else?" He sat waiting, unaware of the energy that was whooshing through his office, lifting Ruby higher and higher so she could explore the outer edges of the great blue eternity inside her mind.

"I'm okay." The air smelled of sage.

Klingston looked suddenly small in his Aeron chair, as though Ruby were viewing him from a great height.

"One more thing," he said. "Bridezilla and Company won't be back for a while. The bride's postponed the wedding."

Good for her! The words were so real, Ruby wondered if someone had uttered them aloud. She had not. And neither had Klingston, who was busying fingering his clicker with one meaty paw.

He glanced up and, misreading the puzzled look on Ruby's face, offered reassurance. "Don't worry about Bridezilla and Company. Forget them. The beta audience will love it. It's good news for the show. The press will go for it. Which means it's good for the reality division. Which is good for the network."

And good for you.

The words hung in the air between them like smog. Klingston didn't care one bit about the guests who came onto her show or anything else except his ratings. Ruby said nothing but held Klingston's gaze.

He was the first to look away. He cleared his throat. "I'm sure Ashley and Sten will work things out."

No thanks to you, Ruby thought. She stood to go. "I'll let you know if I need anything."

The producer's thick eyebrows rose higher onto his shelf of a forehead. Generally, he decided when to end a meeting. It was a Guy thing.

But the balance of power had shifted, and they both knew it. Ruby was, after all, host of the hottest reality show in his stable.

"Good," Klingston said. "Good, good, good."

Ruby left Klingston's office and headed to the elevator, not sure what had just happened. She tried telling herself she was better off without the likes of Charles Begley Hutchinson IV on her set or in her life, given that she suddenly felt like John Wayne. She should be happy. Good riddance.

So why did she feel as if she had just lost her last and best chance to have her very own Relationship Rx?

The scent of sage in the hall was so strong, she expected to see tumbleweeds blowing past the elevator bank. She pressed the call button, wondering how this day could get any weirder.

Ruby got her answer a moment later, when the doors slid open and Kristal stepped out.

She was dressed in slacks and a trench coat today, totally different than last night. That was something. In fact, Kristal didn't look much like an evil temptress at all. She simply looked as though she wished she hadn't just stepped off the elevator and practically run into Ruby.

"I came to pick something up," Kristal said, eyeing Klingston's office.

A million snarky comments came to mind, but Ruby opted to ask a question instead. "What do you need to pick up?"

"A paycheck."

"For what?" But Ruby knew the answer.

"For working Sten Wellingsworth's bachelor party."

"You mean, Klingston hired you?"

Kristal nodded.

Ruby blinked, trying to take it all in. "So . . . ?"

"Klingston arranged the whole thing. He wanted to turn the heat up on your show," Kristal said.

Ruby groaned aloud. Last night in the hot tub had been one big setup, courtesy of The Barbarian. Of course he was responsible. It was as clear as petroglyphs on a cave wall. And she, Ruby, had missed it. She had chosen to blame Hutch instead.

Because she chose to hold on to the past and the old hurt, even though things always worked out for the best in the end. Even though she could choose to learn her life lessons and move on, soaring up high into her own Faraway if she chose to.

But first she had to let go of the old hurt, stop blaming men in general, and move on.

"Whoa? Did you feel that?" Ruby stood stock-still.

"Feel what?" Kristal frowned.

It was then that the lightbulb switched on inside Ruby's head. Not just one lightbulb. It was more like the full pumping power of Con Ed's Big Bertha plant in Astoria, Queens, providing enough juice to light up the entire island of Manhattan through the next millennium.

Ruby got it. The Manly Man voice, the Guy Point of View, whatever. The voice was there, inside her head. Telling her she could no longer blame other people for her problems. And, more important, she didn't have to be perfect anymore. Suddenly, the dream made sense. She, Ruby, was struggling for takeoff. Taking flight. Healing.

"Wow." Ruby squared her shoulders and set her chin. She was no longer the Jilted Bride. Not on the inside. The tabloids could publish what they wished. Ruby blinked. The glare was so bright, she practically needed shades.

Kristal didn't seem to notice. "You know, the only reason Hutch jumped into that tub was so Ashley wouldn't see Sten in there with me. Hutch jumped in at the last minute."

"To keep Ashley from being hurt again," Ruby said slowly, wishing it hadn't taken her so long to figure it out.

But what difference did it make? She had figured it out.

"Right. Hutch would do anything to keep someone from getting hurt. He's a great guy," Kristal said pointedly. "We had some laughs together, but things didn't work out. No hard feelings." She shot Ruby a look that showed she didn't have much patience for women who harbored hard feelings.

At the moment, Ruby couldn't agree more.

"Hutch is a stand-up guy. Any woman would be lucky to have him." Kristal gave Ruby another look.

Ruby saw for the first time that Kristal was in possession of certain qualities that would have been attractive to a Regular Guy like Hutch.

She was the sort of woman a man could relax and have a good time with.

There it was. The voice again. Ruby looked at Kristal. "Did you hear that?"

"Hear what?"

"Never mind," Ruby said, knowing that the Guy voice was only in her mind. She pressed the button to call the elevator. "But thanks." She meant it.

Kristal nodded.

The elevator arrived, and Ruby stepped aboard. "There's something I need to do. Right now."

Timing is key.

Ruby blew past the sidewalk concession stands for once and halled a cab. The rumbling in her stomach had stopped, anyway. Depending on how much packing Hutch needed to do, she might still catch him. But the thought of that toiletry kit, hanging ready on the back of his bathroom door, haunted her.

Traffic crawled slowly enough to make even a diva consider ditching her cab in favor of the No. 7 subway. Almost, but not quite. She finally did give up just east of

Grand Central and ran the rest of the way, no small feat in three-inch Kate Spade heels.

But Ruby was, after all, a native New Yorker.

The doorman waved her up with barely a glance.

As though women raced in, windblown and breathless, to visit Hutch every day.

So what if they did?

There it was again. The Guy voice. And Ruby had to admit, there was no point arguing with it.

She felt an eerie calm when she knocked on Hutch's door.

If things were meant to work out, they would work out.

Chapter Nineteen

"Come on in. It's open," Hutch called.

Only a Texan would do that.

Ruby stepped inside.

The living room looked less lived in than ever, with two battered cases of equipment stacked at the door, ready to go.

"You can grab those and load them," Hutch called. "I'll follow you down with my suitcase in five minutes."

Ruby followed the sound of his voice to the bedroom and paused in the doorway.

He was smoothing the quilt on his bed, the one with interlocking wedding bands. Sensing her presence, he straightened up and turned. "I said I'd be down . . ." His voice faded when he saw Ruby.

"It's not the driver," Ruby said, stating the obvious. "It's me."

192

"Yeah." He swallowed, and his gaze flickered over her, making her aware of her body, and for the first time in her life she didn't take an inventory of how much weight she had gained or what she was wearing or how her thighs looked. Maybe because she knew Hutch thought she was hot no matter what. Or maybe it was the John Wayne voice in her head. Maybe. Whatever.

So they stood there looking at each other for a time, while Ruby noticed he wasn't wearing cowboy boots today. Just plain, sturdy, hardworking lace-ups.

"Sorry," he said in a low voice. "You caught me on my way out."

She couldn't tell whether he was sorry he was on his way out or whether she had caught him at it. "Hutch," she began, taking a step closer.

He froze as if she had hit him with a laser beam.

Up until yesterday Ruby would have said something like, *We need to talk.* But not now. "I made a mistake," she said, "and I came here to fix it."

He shrugged, stuffing his hands into the pockets of his khakis. "Don't worry about it."

Man Speak for *Please don't throw another hissy fit.* Ruby felt for him. She no longer had the stomach for hissy fits herself. So now she stood there, drew in a deep breath, and braced herself for what she was about to do. Something she had never done before. Speak the truth to a Man. "I resented you for what happened to me. I didn't realize it before Ashley and Sten came onto the show, but I was holding a grudge about my own broken engagement." Big, hot, salty tears sprang to Ruby's eyes and spilled down her cheeks. "I guess I got hurt so badly, I blamed everyone else. And I'm sorry."

Hutch watched her, jamming his hands deeper into his pockets, poking his tongue from one side of his cheek to the other in that manly, pensive sort of way.

Ruby got the sense it took all his strength not to rush across the room and rescue her. Funny, the things you noticed about other people when you weren't busy throwing hissy fits.

"It's okay," he said at last. "People make mistakes. I've made a few of my own, I guess. You're forgiven." He grinned.

Now Ruby really felt as if she were soaring ten feet above the ground. And despite the fact that she was starting to cry and her nose was probably turning bright red like Rudolph's and her mascara was taking quite a beating, she couldn't help but smile at him.

Because it felt good to let her feelings out for once instead of holding them in, in a divalike way. And even though it was weird at first, it felt okay to let Hutch see her, messy feelings and all. What was even weirder was the fact that he didn't rush over to try to stop her tears. He just stood there, letting her have her feelings. It was very liberating.

Say what you'd like about Charles Begley Hutchinson IV, but he was the sort of man you could cry in front of and feel okay.

Hutch could take it. He was, after all, the Cowboy Cameraman.

Epilogue

"**S**top the car! Oh, Hutch, stop the car!"

They would be at the main house in less than a mile, but Hutch knew better than to argue with a woman who was yanking his arm half out of its socket. He pulled the rental car to the side of the road, shifted it into park, and got out.

The place was just the way Hutch remembered it, which was a good thing. He had planned to bring Ruby here once they had gotten the formalities out of the way and she had met his parents and all seven sisters.

But Ruby, as usual, had her own ideas. She was already clicking along in her high heels over the river rocks that formed a path through the pea gravel that was the front yard of the chapel.

"Hurry!" she called over her shoulder.

Hutch closed the distance between them in two giant

strides, grabbing her hand and leading her up the wooden steps. Ol' Ruby walked fast, like a real New Yorker, even in those heels. Grinning, he opened the heavy oak door and held it as she stepped inside.

The inside was as dark as a cave after the blazing west Texas sun, and it took Hutch's eyes a moment to adjust. Votive candles flickered from tiny recesses in the plaster walls. The only other illumination came from a skylight set high up in the tongue-and-groove ceiling. Hutch breathed deeply and got a lungful of prairie sage with the slightest hint of incense, the combination of smells that was unique to this place. He let that breath out slowly and took in another.

Ruby skidded to a stop halfway up the aisle, just under the skylight, and looked down at the mosaic embedded in the floor at their feet. "It's here," she breathed.

And it was. Hundreds of gleaming white ceramic tiles in the shape of a bird climbing into a brilliant blue sky, with shafts of gold radiating from its wings.

She raised her gaze to meet his, and Hutch saw something in them that was shining and beautiful not just on the outside but on the inside, and he knew in his heart that bringing Ruby here had been the right thing to do.

"Tell me about this," she whispered, and the sound was soft in the tiny chapel.

Hutch explained the story he'd been told as a little boy, about the mysterious man who passed through these parts on his way down from the Santa Fe Trail. "This man brought his toolbox and stayed here long enough to fire up pieces of clay in a local kiln. He set them into the floor of this chapel and left."

"Where did he go?"

Hutch shrugged. "Nobody knows."

Ruby studied the mosaic. "What does it mean?"

Hutch looked around the tiny chapel, where five generations of Hutchinsons had been baptized and married.

"There are a couple of theories about that," he explained. "I believe it's the myth of the phoenix . . ."

"Rising into the sky from its own ashes." Ruby finished the sentence for him. "Born again."

He nodded and watched her take it all in. She said something about feeling as if she'd been here before, but it was hard for Hutch to follow what she was saying. He couldn't concentrate on anything except the light in Ruby's blue eyes, the way the sunshine lit the gold hair tumbling loose around her shoulders, the way her skin glowed from the inside like alabaster.

He had invited her home to Texas on the spur of the moment after she surprised him at his apartment. He'd gotten the all-clear from the staff doc to go back to the network news division, but in light of recent events, racing back to Iraq would have felt like running away.

Jumping into the hot tub for Sten that night hadn't exactly been throwing himself onto a grenade, but it had squared things with Ashley and put Hutch's demons to rest. So he'd gotten to thinking there were other things he could try, like trading in his video cam for an SLR to take still portraits of the people and place he loved best, right here in west Texas. He'd gone back to his apartment to pack that day, deciding a visit to the old sod was in order.

He'd been about to leave when Ruby popped in. One thing led to another, and here they were. He smiled at her now.

Ruby smiled back, her eyes damp with tears, and Hutch saw that she felt the same way about this place as he did. A New Yorker, barely one hour off the plane. Go figure.

There was no time to think about that right now. His mother would be pretending to fuss with the curtains, watching the long drive up to the house like a hawk on the wing, for one thing.

For another, Ruby was tilting her pretty face up to his in that way that made him forget everything else.

So Hutch did the Manly Man thing, catching Ruby in his arms and kissing her long and hard as though he had been waiting all his life for her to come along and be his own True Match.

And so he had.